Saltwater Kisses

A Billionaire Love Story

KRISTA LAKES

To my Daddy.
I'll always be your little girl.

CONTENTS

Chapter One   1

Chapter Two   11

Chapter Three   27

Chapter Four   37

Chapter Five   46

Chapter Six   55

Chapter Seven   63

Chapter Eight   72

Chapter Nine   78

Chapter Ten   88

Chapter Eleven   92

Chapter Twelve   101

Chapter Thirteen   115

Chapter Fourteen   128

Chapter Fifteen   140

Chapter Sixteen   149

Chapter Seventeen   156

Chapter Eighteen   169

Chapter Nineteen   174

Chapter Twenty   184

Chapter Twenty-one   193

Chapter Twenty-two   200

Epilogue   209

ACKNOWLEDGMENTS

A special thank you to everyone involved in this amazing process. You know who you are and that I am eternally grateful.

I'd especially like to thank all the participants of the Insatiable Reads Tour. It is through their support that this novel was created.

CHAPTER ONE

I stepped off the plane. A wave of humid air hit me, the smell of salt and flowers blowing through my hair and ruffling my clothes. I took a deep breath, memorizing the smell. It was the smell of the start of a great vacation. I stepped carefully down the stair ramp, feeling like a movie star as I exited the small plane and followed a red carpet off the runway and to the small terminal. I couldn't wipe the grin off my face to save my life.

The airport terminal was open to the Caribbean air. It seemed strange to me at first, until I realized that the weather was always nice enough here that they wouldn't need to have double-paned windows. It was a foreign concept to someone like me who had always lived in a place that required heating and cooling throughout the year. My windows in Iowa were only open in the late spring and early fall due to the weather outside which was either too hot or too cold. I loved the idea of having windows open year round, the weather always nice.

My bags were already circling the small baggage carousel, the benefit of being the only plane at a small airport. The bag clicked behind me on the tile floor as I looked around for my ride to the hotel. I found a well-dressed man with large aviator glasses holding up a sign with my name on it: Emma LaRue. I must have looked like someone ready for vacation because he started smiling at me as soon as he saw me. Must have been the grin plastered on my face and the big eyes trying to take it all in.

"Ms. LaRue?" he asked, a lilting accent twisting my name into something exotic. "I'm Felipe. If you need anything during your stay here, please just let me know." I smiled and nodded excitedly as he took my bags and ushered me towards a waiting fancy town car. I felt spoiled as he opened the door and I slid into the soft leather seat. The air was running and the car felt cold after the tropical warmth of the airport.

Felipe entered the driver's seat and easily maneuvered the car out onto the main road. I pressed my nose against the tinted glass like a little kid, watching this beautiful world zoom past. Palm trees and plants that only grew in greenhouses lined the road, green things growing wild against the bright blue sky.

"Is this your first time to the island?" Felipe asked, smiling in the mirror at my amazement.

"Yes — I've almost never left Iowa," I said, never taking my eyes from the window.

"Iowa? What is in Iowa?" Felipe asked, his accent making my home state sound like a foreign country.

"Just pigs and corn," I said with a laugh.

"Pigs and corn. We have only fish and coconuts here. Hopefully you will find it to your liking," he said as he turned the car smoothly. I could see the ocean in the distance now, the sunlight making it gleam along the horizon.

"I like fish and coconuts," I said and he laughed.

"Is that why you are vacationing here?"

"Well, I actually won this trip. There was a contest on the radio. I never win anything, but I somehow won this," I said staring at the gleaming horizon. I had never seen the ocean, and even from this distance, I could only stare in wonder. It was so big and beautiful, even from far away. I could barely believe I would see it up close.

I was sure I was going to wake up at any moment. My favorite radio station had run a contest for an all-expenses-paid vacation to the exclusive tropical paradise resort on Ocean Key. I had called in on a whim, and fast-forward two months, here I was. It still felt surreal.

"You must be very lucky if you won a trip to Ocean Blue Resort," Felipe said as he drove past an ornate sign bearing the name. A waterfall cascaded next to bright blue tile letters proclaiming the name from the road. It looked expensive and fancy.

"It might be the universe trying to even out my usual bad luck," I said. Felipe laughed, as if I had made a joke. I smiled, but it wasn't a joke to me. Things never seemed to go my way. I had this horrible suspicion that this was merely an elaborate joke at my expense. I was going to arrive at the resort and my room would be occupied, or I'll find that I was actually responsible for the bill and would end up paying for everything. That would be the kind of luck I usually had. Not this *good* kind of luck.

Felipe pulled the car up to the entrance of the resort. I stepped out and felt my jaw drop. The main entrance was huge and open to the air. High above marble floors beautiful gossamer fabric hung in giant loops fluttering gently in the soft ocean breeze. Big, comfy chairs adorned the lobby and a babbling creek ran along the side complete with several small wooden foot bridges. A beautiful bar in the corner served drinks in colorful glasses. I could see only top shelf liquor.

I gulped. This was by far the nicest place I had ever been in. It really was a tropical paradise. There was no way I would have been able to afford a place like this on my vet tech salary. I wondered how much the radio station paid for all this, or rather what connections they had that allowed them offer a free vacation in a place like this. I shook my head at the thought of all that money and power.

"You must be Ms. LaRue. I am Anna," said a female voice with a soft British accent. A woman in a linen sleeveless dress stepped forward, a smile highlighting her tropical features. I smiled nervously and nodded. "We've been expecting you. If you would follow me to check-in please." She smiled again and gestured towards a glass-enclosed office in the corner of the lobby. I picked up the handle to my suitcase, but she waved a hand to stop me. "The bellhop will take it to your room for you. You are on vacation, Ms. LaRue," she said as she smiled, her white teeth beautiful against her dark skin. A man in a navy-blue uniform hurried over and reached for my suitcase. I let him take it and he gave a curt nod and placed it on a luggage trolley. "If you will please follow me?"

Anna opened the door to her office and cold air-conditioned air flowed out. I stepped inside and sat gingerly down on a leather chair.

"I just need your signature here to indicate that you are checking in. Music Radio Inc. has already covered all charges," Anna said handing me a pen and an important looking document. "I will need your signature on the next page as well. It is simply a liability waiver and that you agree not to damage the property."

I scanned the document quickly, looking over the legal words and evaluating. Anna waited patiently as I read every word, her eyes only confused for a moment. *Most people must not read this*, I thought, but I wanted to know exactly what I was signing. The control freak in me had to make sure I was in control of what I agreed to. It was the standard legal agreement I was expecting, so I signed it with a flourish.

"Excellent. You will be staying in Cabana Four. Here is your identification bracelet. This simply notifies staff that you are staying at the resort and will allow you to access all the dining facilities, beverage stations, and the spa," Anna said as she handed me a bright pink rubber bracelet. She helped me fasten it as she continued. "You have complete access to all the amenities of the resort. If you need anything, please ask any of our staff. I have included a packet with all the information you will need for your stay."

I peeked in the envelope. There was a certificate for a beach massage, some rental vouchers for water sports equipment, and menus for the different restaurants on the resort. I tried to keep my fingers from shaking; this was really happening. I was having a vacation that people only dream about. That stupid happy smile crept back onto my face.

"Well, everything is done here. Are you ready to go to your cabana?" Anna asked as she filed the paperwork. She laughed gently at my animated nod. "Follow me, please."

Anna led me out of the lobby to a pristine white golf cart. Felipe winked at me from the driver's seat as I climbed in next to him. Anna wished me a happy stay and I hung on tight as Felipe started down the beautifully gardened path.

"Enjoying yourself so far?" he asked, smiling at my obvious excitement.

"I can't believe it's real. This place is beautiful," I said. My eyes darted around the resort as he drove me towards the beach. Everywhere I looked were big beautiful trees and tropical flowers. It was exactly what I thought a tropical paradise should look like. The movies, for once, were right.

"There are three pools on the property. The one closest to the main restaurant is where all the activities occur. We have water aerobics, pool volleyball, and other games throughout the day for anyone interested. The beach is open at all times, as are the pools," Felipe explained as we drove by a giant pool with a swim-up bar. He continued on about the five restaurants, the evening entertainment shows, the eight bars, and the myriad of other opportunities the resort offered, but I had stopped listening. I could see the ocean.

It was so big. And blue. And probably the most beautiful thing I had ever seen in my life.

I was born and raised in a small town just outside of Des Moines, Iowa. I hadn't had any opportunities to go far from home. The most exotic place I had ever been was Chicago with my high school honors society. The biggest body of water I had seen up until this point was the Mississippi and Lake Michigan, but this was so much better.

Felipe pulled up next to a small tropical cabin and stepped out to grab my bag. I sat in the golf cart mesmerized by the water. It was a shade of blue that made me want to dive in and never leave. The sound of the waves lapping the shore was better than any recording could ever be, and the smell of water, salt, and sun threatened to overwhelm me with joy.

"Miss? Would you like to see your room?" Felipe asked, touching my shoulder. I blushed and stood.

"Sorry. I've never seen the ocean before," I said. He laughed and gestured to the thatched building, guiding me toward the door.

"I forget that people have never seen it before," he said. He turned towards the blue horizon and peered out at the water, a smile on his face. "It is beautiful. I suppose I would feel the same if I ever saw snow," he said as he stepped up on the porch and opened the door.

"You've never seen snow? How strange," I said as I entered the room. I immediately forgot what I was going to say. If the lobby was beautiful, the room was opulent. The main room had a leather couch and giant TV, but the windows opened out onto the ocean. I took slow steps into the bedroom. A king-sized four-poster bed dominated the room. A gentle breeze blew through the big open bay windows, ruffling the bedspread. I could hear the ocean as though I were sitting on the beach. I glanced towards the bathroom and could see a giant tub and shower that looked like it could hold four.

"What do you think, Ms. LaRue from Iowa?" Felipe asked as he set my suitcase down in the bedroom. I couldn't find the words to answer, and I turned to face him, my mouth hanging open. He laughed and patted my shoulder.

"Enjoy yourself. You say these things never happen to you? Then this is an adventure. Let yourself take risks and have the time of your life. You only live once," Felipe said, seriously, but his dark eyes sparkled with amusement as I contemplated his words.

"This is going to be the best adventure," I said slowly, looking out onto the blue ocean. I would never get the chance to go someplace like this again. Not on my salary. I decided right then that I was going to be fearless while I was here. This was going to be the best vacation in the history of vacations.

There was nothing I wasn't going to do.

I spent the rest of the day exploring the resort. Between the pools, the restaurants, the spa, and the gym, I was never going to want to leave. The excitement finally got to me and I crashed into the incredibly comfortable bed immediately after dinner and fell into a deep sleep.

The next day, I was up almost before the sun was, excited and anxious to play in the blue water just outside my cabana house. I threw on my swimsuit and a sundress and skipped out to the main restaurant for breakfast. I sat out on the patio, drinking in the cloudless blue sky, the aquamarine water, and the soft calls of strange birds. I tried mashed plantains, mistaking them for mashed potatoes at first. They were delicious, with a taste similar to potatoes, but with a smoother texture. They didn't taste anything like bananas and I found myself going back for a second serving.

After breakfast, I walked around to the pool, thinking I would sit by the edge and have easy access to the bar and the water, but as soon as I sat down, I changed my mind. I couldn't hear the ocean anymore, and I realized I could sit by a pool at home. I really just wanted to stay on the beach all day.

"Can I get a drink to go?" I asked the bartender by the pool. "A piña colada please." It was still early, but if I was going to be on the beach, I wasn't sure if I was going to be willing to get up to get one later.

"Of course," the bartender said. I loved the accents everyone had here. He looked over and somehow read my mind. "Are you going to the beach?"

I nodded. He must have seen me sit down only to stand up again. He reached under the bar while the blender whirled my drink and pulled out a small clicker device.

"Here, use this on the beach. When you want a drink, just press the button and someone will bring you your last order."

"I press this and someone will bring me a piña colada? On the beach? I am never leaving this place!" I grinned as I took the small device. He laughed and handed me my drink, complete with a little umbrella. I thanked him and headed back to the beach, snagging a towel from the pool towel cart. Today was going to be amazing.

≈ஓ❧ ❧ஓ≈

CHAPTER TWO

I stretched out on my towel, and then sat up, digging my feet into the sand at the edge of my towel. The sand burned a little, but the heat felt so good on my skin. I couldn't believe how much I was enjoying being on the beach. The ocean sparkled in the tropical sun, the sand glowed with sunlight. Gulls called in the distance, but the constant breathing of the ocean was all I wanted to hear. I never wanted to stop hearing it.

I was almost alone on the beach. A single figure walked along the waterline to my right, and the couple staying in the cabana next to mine played in the water to my left. Other than that, the beach was empty as most of the resort guests preferred the pool with the swim up bar. I didn't quite understand why they all preferred being on display in a crowded pool when the ocean was right here, but I was happy to have the beach to myself.

I smoothed the front of my swimsuit self-consciously. It was expensive, but the 1940s style cut flattered my curves. "You just have real curves," a friend had once said when I complained about how I looked. I was never going to be model thin. I did try to take care of myself, but I was never quite happy with my body shape. I tried not to let it bother me, but swimsuits were always dangerous ground. I thought this swimsuit accentuated the curves I liked and hid the ones I didn't. So far, it was worth every penny.

I watched the couple splash for a moment, the girl shrieking with delight as the man tried to dunk her under the water. I felt a surge of jealousy. I had technically won a trip for two, but I had come alone.

I lived by myself, had no boyfriend, and my older sister who was supposed to come with me had gotten appendicitis and had to cancel at the last minute. It was easy enough to cancel the reservation for her, but it meant that no one else was able to get the time off to go with me. I was on my own for this trip. I sighed and turned away from the happy couple. Valentine's Day had only been a couple of weeks ago, and I didn't want another reminder that I was alone.

I looked towards the solitary figure in the other direction. It was a man, at least good looking from the distance, but unhappy about something. It was subtle, but the way he kicked at the waves and clenched his hands, I could tell he was not enjoying his vacation. I wasn't sure how that was possible in a place like this, but I wasn't about to let a stranger ruin my good mood. He was walking slowly towards my spot on the beach, lost in his own thoughts.

I pressed the small clicker the bar had given me for "beach service", knowing they would bring me a fresh piña colada in minutes. This really was a slice of heaven.

"Help! Somebody, help! *HELP!*" A scream came from the water, high pitched and full of fear. I jerked up, knocking my sunglasses off my face. The girl was screaming and thrashing in the water. My first thought was a shark, but the water was still crystal blue. She was struggling with the man's limp body towards shore, screaming as she battled the waves.

I was up in a heartbeat and racing towards her to help. Out of the corner of my eye I could see the solitary man running in the same direction I was headed. I crashed into the shallow waves, the first touch of the warm water surprising me. I had expected it to be cold, but it felt more like bathwater. I reached the girl quickly and grabbed hold of her boyfriend's arm to help drag him into shore.

"What happened?" I shouted as we pulled his dead weight through the water.

"I don't know! One minute he was under the water, and the next he was just floating there. I thought he was just playing, but, oh God..." she cried softly. The solitary man reached us, not even breathing hard despite the fact he had sprinted down the beach. Between the three of us, we maneuvered the unconscious man onto the beach, his feet still in the waves as I bent to check his pulse.

I couldn't find it. I wasn't sure if I was too excited

and was missing it, or if I really couldn't find one. Either way, I knew what I had to do. It was more instinct than actual thought; I placed one hand on the other and began pumping his chest, humming an old Bee Gee's song under my breath. The girl started screaming again and Solitary Man quickly grabbed her and took her up higher on the beach, asking her questions. I could barely hear them, like they were in a far away dream as I concentrated on making my thrusts deep and even.

"Does he have any heart conditions?"

"I don't know... wait, yes! He said it wasn't a problem though!"

"Is he on any medications? Even stuff that he wasn't prescribed?"

"No, no... Well, he took something today. A little blue pill. It's our first vacation together and we didn't think it would cause any harm! Oh god, why did I let him take it?"

The man underneath my fingers suddenly lurched and gasped. I quickly rolled him on his side, just in time, as he vomited salt water and whatever he had for lunch all over the beach. I rocked back on my heels, suddenly light headed. My shoulders and back ached; I hadn't realized how hard I had been pushing. The girl was screaming again, but this time with joy as she rushed over to check on him.

A uniformed man came running towards me carrying a big red medical bag. Another man carrying an orange back-board was hot on his heels. I stood up and backed away slowly in a haze, letting the professionals take over. They spoke quickly between themselves, efficiently transferring the man onto the back-board and hooking up a blood pressure cuff and other monitoring devices. Before I had cleared my thoughts enough to understand what was going on, they were already halfway up the beach to a waiting ambulance. They passed by a confused looking waiter with a piña colada walking towards my empty towel on the beach.

I brushed the hair out of my eyes, suddenly realizing I had lost my sunglasses. I glanced around the beach, but couldn't see them anywhere. A kernel of irritation welled up inside my chest; I really liked those sunglasses. I kicked at the sand before realizing that my sunglasses weren't important. I giggled a little; I had just saved a man's life, but my issue with the day was about my missing sunglasses. People lose sunglasses all the time, but very few people randomly save a stranger on their vacation.

"That was amazing," a deep voice said by my shoulder. I spun around quickly to see Solitary Man smiling at me.

"Oh, um, thanks. I didn't even really have time to think about it to be honest. I just reacted," I said, a little flustered. Up close, he was really handsome. Like movie star handsome. He had a white t-shirt that did nothing to hide his muscles and dark blue swim trunks that looked expensive. He ran a hand through sandy hair, his eyes twinkling at me.

"Well, I think you saved his life. Not a bad thing to tell the folks at home about your vacation. You did really well," he said. His eyes were focused solely on me, like I could be the center of his world. I fidgeted with my foot in the sand, embarrassed by his praise.

"Thank you. You helped. You kept his girlfriend from completely freaking out," I said quickly. I could still feel my heart pounding a million miles a minute and I wasn't completely sure the whole thing hadn't been a crazy dream. Adventure never happened to me. I was always the one who came in five minutes after the excitement ended, not the person living it. Once again everything felt surreal.

"I think it was his wife. She had a big diamond on her finger," he said with a smile. "I'm Jack by the way. Jack Saunders."

"Emma. Emma LaRue," I replied and shook his outstretched hand. His skin was warm and his grip firm. I felt a strange tingle run through my fingers as we touched, like we were completing a circuit. He smiled and repeated my name, still holding onto my hand.

"Emma. Well, it is very nice to meet you, Emma. Are you staying at the resort here?" He asked. I nodded and held up my other wrist with the pink bracelet.

"Yup. How about you?"

"No, I am staying at a house on the beach a little further down," he said, jerking his head back in the direction he had come from. He still hadn't let go of my hand and I wasn't about to complain. I found myself wanting to touch even more of him.

"Oh, that must be nice. The houses I saw on the way in looked very nice," I said, instantly sounding dumb in my head. I needed to find a new adjective. I let myself off the hook for it though. I was still a little shell shocked. He sighed and let go of my hand.

"I am actually trying to escape it right now," he said, his smile gone. It was like the sun had dipped behind a cloud when he stopped smiling.

"It can't be that bad," I said, hoping he would smile again.

"I came with someone, and I thought we were going to have a good time, but it has been miserable. I couldn't stay in the house with her a second longer," he said with a grimace.

"Girlfriend?" I asked, trying to keep the disappointment out of my voice. If he was here with someone, then I probably would never see him again. I had only known him for less than five minutes, but I never wanted him to leave.

"Secretary. I thought maybe the cliché would work, but it's no fun out of the office," he said. He shook his head and shrugged. I nodded. He had a secretary. Those swim shorts probably were as expensive as they looked.

"So you just left her?"

"She's out admiring the pool boy and still hung over from last night. It hasn't been the best vacation of my life," he said. "Our conversation has been the most civil one I've had all day," he said looking directly into my eyes.

"That is no vacation. Vacations are supposed to be fun. You know, maybe even save a life or something," I said coyly. I was never very good at flirting, but I didn't want him to leave. I wanted to talk to him all day. I asked the first thing I could think of to get him to stay, "You want a drink?"

He laughed. "A drink sounds great."

We walked over to my towel, the piña colada melting quickly in the sun. I smiled sheepishly at the melted drink, and bent to pick up the clicker from my towel.

"I'll get you a fresh one," I said quickly.

"We can split this one until it comes, You look like you could use a sip. Besides, I'm in no hurry; I'm on vacation," he said, settling into the sand and taking a big sip of the slushy drink. I hit the clicker and sat down next to him. He handed me the drink and I took a small sip off the side.

"How did the ambulance get here so quick?" I asked. Now that a couple of minutes had passed and the adrenaline was wearing down, I felt the weight of what had happened hit me. I was glad I was sitting. I took another bigger sip. I was sure I was going to wake up any moment. How could this be happening? I had saved someone's life and was now sitting next to the most gorgeous man I had ever seen. My life was not this exciting or this good.

"I called it. I heard her screaming and then you took off like a bat out of hell," he said nonchalantly as he gently took the glass from my hand and took another sip.

"You have a phone that works out here? That must cost an arm and a leg. My phone company said mine wouldn't work on the island," I said. He handed me the drink and I took a big sip this time. My nerves still felt frayed, but with him sitting next to me, it still felt too dream-like for me to worry about it.

"The downside of my business; even on vacation,

I have to carry a phone." He took the drink back and took another swallow. It was almost half gone at this point.

"What do you do?"

"I work for my father's company. What do you do?" he said, dodging my actual question. He looked at me like I should know who he was, but I didn't press him for more. He was on vacation and didn't want to talk about work. I could understand that.

"I'm a vet tech," I answered and reached for the drink.

"So, you work with animals?" He asked, waiting for me to finish swallowing so I could answer.

"Yup. I love it. I'm actually in the process of applying for Veterinary School," I said proudly.

"So you want to be a vet? That sounds like a great job. I wanted to be a doctor when I was a kid," he finished off the last of the drink and set the glass in the sand. "But with my dad's business, that was never really an option. I hope you do it though. If you can save animals like you save people, you'll be great."

"Thanks. I sure hope so," I said with a smile. He glanced over at me, his brows darkening slightly as he thought of something.

"If you don't mind me asking, how can you afford this vacation? I can't imagine vet techs make enough to go on vacations to an exclusive resort very often," he said. His outward appearance never changed, but a current of tension wound through him, as though he suspected something.

"You want to know my age and weight too?" I asked with a smirk. He managed to look slightly abashed, but obviously still wanted an answer. It seemed strange, but it was a question I would ask if I were on a super expensive resort too. I was an interloper on this island.

"I actually won this trip — a radio station call in thing. My sister was supposed to come with me, but she got sick at the last minute. There is no way I would ever be able to afford anything like this otherwise," I said before realizing I had just told him I was poor and very alone here. I smiled nervously and hoped he didn't notice.

"So you're here alone?" he asked, raising his eyebrows. No such luck there.

"Um, well, the resort is keeping track of me, so I'm not really alone," I tried to backpedal. A quick pulse of terror pushed through me, but I fought it down. Telling things like that to a complete stranger, no matter how good looking, was not a good way to stay safe. My dad would have killed me if he knew I was telling people I was here by myself.

"No, no, that's good. I was afraid you were here with a husband or boyfriend."

"Husband? No. With work and applying to vet schools, I haven't even had time to go on a date in months," I said. I hoped he didn't think I sounded pathetic. He laughed and leaned back on his elbows, the tension gone from him again.

"I hear you on the too busy thing. Why do you think I came with my secretary? She's the only person I see on a daily basis I felt like I could ask," he laughed and then scowled at the thought of his secretary. "I thought there would be more to her away from work, but she is so boring. She's almost too perfect if you know what I mean."

I laughed and nodded. "I'm sorry she is ruining your vacation."

"Well, suddenly I don't feel like it is ruined." He smiled and I doubted it was possible for him to be more handsome. "Especially now that we have another drink," he said with a wink as the resort waiter appeared with a fresh piña colada. He thanked the waiter and handed him a couple of dollar bills. The waiter smiled and promised to bring more whenever we buzzed again. I waited for him to leave before turning to Jack.

"I didn't know we were supposed to tip them. When they said 'all expenses paid' I thought that included tips," I said, mortified. My face felt on fire with my blush. Jack laughed and handed me the drink.

"You don't have to tip them. I did because I'm not a guest here and I would like him to keep bringing us drinks," he said with a tilt of his head.

"That's good. For a minute there, I was thinking I was the worst guest ever. So, you wanted to be a doctor?" I asked, changing the subject and hoping my blush would fade.

"Yeah. I liked the idea of helping people and really making a difference in someone's life. Like what you did for the guy on the beach. I would do that every day if I could," he said.

"I just realized I never got his name. I hope he is alright," I said playing with the edge of my towel. "So what stopped you from following your dream?"

"My parents. Specifically, my dad's company," he sighed. "I am their oldest child, so it was made pretty clear that I would someday take over the company. I don't really have the option not to at this point."

"That's too bad. Maybe you could find a way to combine it? I don't know what your dad's company does, but maybe there is a way to help people with it. Or, you could always volunteer or donate to something that does," I sipped the drink before handing it back to Jack.

"No one has ever made it sound so easy. You are the first person to actually make me believe I could do something like that," he said softly. He smiled, his eyes lighting up. They were a combination of green and brown, a hazel that couldn't decide what color it wanted to be. A girl could lose herself in those eyes.

"Anytime," I said with a smile. He handed me the cold glass and I sipped on the sweet liquid. "You said you were the oldest? How many siblings do you have?"

"Just one. A younger brother."

"Are you close?" I took another sip before setting the drink carefully in the sand.

"Not really. He's almost seven years younger than me, and the expectations my parents have for him are very different than the ones they have for me." Jack shifted in the sand, a sadness in the subtle motion.

"They don't expect much of him, but they expect everything of you."

Jack looked at me surprised. "That's it exactly! How did you figure that out?"

"Easy. That's how it is in my world too. Only, I'm

the younger sibling." I shrugged and Jack nodded.

"What does your sister do that makes them not expect much of you?" Jack asked.

"She works in the ER as a physician assistant. My dad is a dentist and I think he kind of assumed that his kids would both go into some sort of medicine. I'm not exactly following that trend."

"You're going into animal medicine, doesn't that count?" He leaned back on his elbows, the shirt barely disguising a perfect six pack. I looked out to the ocean so I wouldn't stare.

"Apparently not enough. It's not a big deal though." I suddenly realized that this was a more serious topic than I had intended and I quickly added, "I didn't mean to put my problems on you. I just meant to say that I understand the family dynamic."

"You're fine. It is actually nice to hear it from the other side. My brother and I don't get the chance to talk much. I've always felt a little guilty about it. I think he has a hard time with it sometimes. More drink?" He held up the nearly empty glass and I nodded, clicking the little button for another.

It felt so peaceful sitting on the beach with Jack. It was like we had known each other forever, like we had always been friends. He had an easygoing charm that made it easy to talk to him, and his laugh made my insides melt. We passed the drink back and forth, ordered another, and then another, talking and laughing.

We talked about everything and nothing at the same time. Our conversation drifted easily from topic to topic, from the weather to our childhoods to what we wanted from the future. It was like catching up with an old friend who really did want to know how life was going. I learned that Jack came from a wealthy family and he was expected to take over his father's company in the next year. It sounded like this was going to be his last vacation for a long while. He was very careful never to say what his company was, and I didn't pry. He grew up with privilege and was fascinated by my stories of growing up "normal."

"I can't imagine your life," he said lying back on the sand. He closed his eyes and obviously tried to imagine it. "Used cars, paying rent, ramen noodles, no one hounding you for money all the time... it sounds great."

"No, we get hounded for money all the time, but we actually owe people the money, and don't have it," I said. He laughed and opened his eyes to look at me as I spoke. "I can't imagine your life — no worries about what bill to pay first, expensive clothes, vacations like this," I gestured to the beach. "Want to switch for a little while?"

Jack rolled onto his side, propped his head on his elbow, and smiled at me. The sun was beginning to set, and the soft reds and golds highlighted his features and glinted off his hair. I felt my breath go short. I had never met a man with a smile like that; I would have followed him around like a puppy for that smile. I felt my cheeks go red and I dropped my eyes, pretending the sand was fascinating.

"Would you be interested in joining me for dinner tonight?" Jack asked, his eyes still trained on my face. I couldn't help it, but my cheeks went redder. I was interested in doing anything with him.

"Won't your secretary mind?"

"I think she is going to be finishing her vacation without me. I think I will be eating here at the resort — I am enjoying your company," he said. I glanced up and saw his eyes were almost golden in the setting sun, and completely serious.

"Sure," I said slowly. Normal me would have found a reason to back out. Normal me would have been afraid. Vacation me wanted the adventure. Vacation me wasn't about to let an opportunity to have dinner with a gorgeous man pass by because I was scared. Besides, what's the worst that could happen? "I'll have to let the resort know."

"I'll call the resort and set it up. It shouldn't be a problem. By the way, you should put some sunscreen on tomorrow. I think your cheeks might be burning," he said as he sat up. Small flecks of sand stuck to his skin and shirt as he stood up. They sparkled in the setting sun, and glistened like falling jewels as he brushed them off. He pulled a phone out of his pocket and searched through a contacts list before putting it to his ear. I was right outside my cabana house, so I stood up and grabbed the towel and clicker. I quickly went to my porch and ducked inside to change for dinner. Everything was going so well. I was taking a handsome man to dinner, and who knew where the night could end up.

CHAPTER THREE

I ran a brush through my long dark hair and grimaced in the mirror at the sand creature looking back. I looked like I had spent the day on the beach, but I didn't have time to clean up. *Besides,* I told myself, *he's been looking at you all day. He doesn't care that you look like a beach-bum.* I grabbed a sundress hanging in my closet and a pair of flip-flop sandals before heading back out. Jack was waiting patiently by the porch step, staring out at the ocean and the setting sun.

Jack turned at the sound of the door and smiled his brilliant smile as I walked towards him. My knees felt weak; a girl could get hurt by that smile.

"You look great," he said honestly. I bit my lip and blushed again.

"Thanks," I said as he offered his elbow to me. I wrapped my arm around his, feeling like a princess in a story book. I liked the way he felt, his arm strong and solid under mine as we walked out of the sand and into the resort.

Twilight was slowly taking over the resort, the sun's rays quickly fading in streams of red and gold that played across the sand and reflected off the water. The pool gleamed like a bright ruby as a couple splashed in its jeweled depths. Small lights twinkled in the palm trees lining the paths to the various areas on the resort. The entire world seemed to glow with excitement and romance. Everywhere I looked, I could see dark romantic corners for lovers to hide, and laughing couples stealing kisses in the fading light. For the first time in a long while, I wasn't envious of the lovers.

Jack kept me laughing as we walked easily towards the restaurant. The wind blew warm across my face and ruffled my skirt, the smell of food drifted out to compel hungry vacationers to eat. He seemed to know where he was going so I let him lead. He guided me carefully past other guests, his hand on the small of my back, directing me where to go as if we were dancing. He walked with confidence and people seemed to step out of his way without realizing it. He didn't seem to notice anyone but me as we headed into the restaurant bearing the island flag.

We were quickly led to a cozy table in the corner. As we settled into the wooden chairs and opened our menus, our conversation paused easily as we decided what to eat. I hoped Jack couldn't hear my stomach growling. I hadn't had much to eat after breakfast other than the piña coladas on the beach and I didn't think that counted as a true meal. I picked a Caribbean jerk chicken with some sort of sweet potato side, and peeked over my menu at Jack. He was deep in thought as he perused the menu, his brows furrowing gently as he made his decision, but his body looked relaxed in the chair. His eyes were dark in the dim light of the restaurant, but something about them drew me into them like a moth to a flame. He looked up and caught me staring and I felt my face go hot again.

"What?" he asked with a grin. "Do I have something in my teeth?"

"No! No..." I scrunched my face and shook my head. "I am having a hard time believing that you are actually here, that today actually happened."

Jack looked at me a little strangely, tensing up noticeably. I realized that I sounded a little crazy and quickly added, "It's not every day you save a man from a heart attack. On top of that, I had an amazing four-hour long conversation with a complete stranger. This doesn't exactly happen in my normal life." With that, Jack seemed to relax back into his chair.

"Isn't that what vacations are for? To have experiences that you don't usually have in your everyday life?" he asked putting his menu down. I bit my bottom lip before answering.

"I suppose so. Vacations are for experiences we don't usually have in our everyday lives. Most people don't get to lounge around and eat bonbons all day, so that is a vacation for them. I don't usually save people's lives and meet handsome strangers who take me to dinner, so that's my vacation," I said.

"Ah, so you think I'm handsome then?" He grinned impishly at me and leaned back in his chair. I felt my cheeks heat again and I hoped the lighting was dim enough so it wasn't too obvious. I could feel his eyes searching my face, waiting for some reaction.

"I should have known better than to stroke your ego," I said, shaking my head. I hoped he would find it coy and not see the embarrassment all over my face. He laughed, a boyish sound that made me want to laugh too.

"You have a magic about you, Emma. I believe every word you say, and I rarely believe anyone," he said as he leaned forward. His eyes caught the light from the small

28

candle on the table and reflected in a million shades of brown and green. I couldn't breathe. I didn't want to. He leaned back and released me from the spell of his eyes. "So, tell me why you want to become a veterinarian," he commanded.

I relaxed, glad he had changed the subject. "It's something I have wanted to do since I was a kid. I love animals," I answered automatically. It was the answer I gave everyone who asked.

"There is more to it than that. You have something more driving you than simply 'I love animals'," he said.

My smile faded from my face. "When I was a kid, my dog got hit by a car. He ran out in the street to chase a ball I had thrown. I held him in my arms as he died, and I didn't know what to do. I promised myself that I wouldn't let that happen again." The words came out of my mouth before I had time to take them back. I never told anyone that story. Ever. It was too personal, showed too much of my weaknesses. Somehow, he had gotten it out of me without even a hesitation.

"That is a much better reason," he said quietly.

"No one believes that I'll be able to do it. I've always gotten good grades and done well in school, but for some reason, no one thinks I'm ever going to be good enough," I said looking at my napkin. He was somehow drawing answers out of me like water from a well.

"No one thinks I am going to be able to run my father's company as well as he did. I'm afraid they might be right," he answered almost more to himself than to me. For a brief moment, the facade of complete control and confidence he emanated faltered.

"That's exactly how I feel," I whispered. Our eyes met and we both smiled. We shared a secret now. Only it didn't feel like a secret. It felt like us saying out loud the truth we both knew in our hearts. As I looked across the table at him, we had no secrets. I knew I could tell him anything.

"Tell me a secret," I said. He blinked twice and then frowned slightly.

"Why?"

"Because we're strangers. Haven't you ever noticed that people can tell a complete stranger something they would barely admit to themselves? It's because there is no judgment and no life consequence. I can tell from your fancy phone and nice clothes that you belong in a place like this." I waved my hand around at the expensive decorations of the resort. "I don't belong here, and when this week is over, I will be going back to my boring, discount-brand life. When we go back to our real lives, we won't accidentally run into one another on the street or at the supermarket. You can tell me anything, and there will be no consequence."

"I wish I could believe you," he said. His lips pressed together and he aged in the dim light. "There is always a consequence. Always."

"I give you my solemn promise to never breathe a word of any of our conversations to anyone without your permission," I said smiling. I wanted to know more about him; anything and everything. He eyed me carefully, obviously weighing my promise in his mind. He wanted to trust me, but something was keeping him in check.

"What would you like to eat this evening?" a young waitress interrupted politely. Jack kept looking at me, trying to decide if I would actually keep my promise.

"I'll have the jerked chicken please," I told her, handing her my menu. She wrote it down on a slip of paper and turned expectantly towards Jack.

"The special please," he said handing her the menu. He smiled up at her before asking, "Can I borrow your pen and paper?"

The waitress frowned for a moment, surprised by his

request, but she shrugged and gave him the next blank page from her small notebook and the pen. He thanked her and she smiled and went to place our order.

"What are you doing?" I asked as he began scribbling on the paper. He finished quickly and handed me the now full page and the pen.

I, Emma LaRue, hereby swear never to reveal any part of this conversation with Jack Saunders to anyone without his direct, written permission.

The words were hard to read in his messy handwriting, but I understood the message.

"With handwriting like that, you should have been a doctor," I said as I examined the words. "I want to clarify the conditions first. It only applies to things said at this table and you have to sign the same promise on the back of this paper."

Jack grinned and nodded. I bent over the tiny paper and signed it, then turned it over and duplicated the words on the other side before handing it to Jack. He signed it with a flourish and stuck the paper in his pocket.

"I wish I didn't have to run my father's company. I wish I could get out of his shadow and be successful in my own right," he said slowly, his eyes glued to my face, waiting to see my reaction.

"Do you want to tell me what your father's company does?" I asked, feeling a little confused.

"If you don't know, then I don't want to tell you," he said with a smile. "It is too refreshing to not have to talk business."

"Okay. You want to get away from your father. That isn't much of a secret," I said, unimpressed.

"It would be if you knew him... Alright, I'll give you a better secret." He paused, thinking about it for a moment. Suddenly, his eyes lowered, shame crossing his face. "When I was fourteen, I stole a car," he said. He smiled when I raised my eyebrows at him. "My father and I were at the country club and we were arguing. I wanted to get away from him so badly I stole a car from the valet."

"What happened after that?" I asked, intrigued.

"I crashed it. Four blocks away I ran it into a lamp post. My father was furious, but instead of punishing me or turning me in to the police, he paid the owner of the car and made the whole thing disappear. To this day we still haven't spoken about it," he said. He picked up his water glass and took a sip, his eyes watching me to see what I was going to say.

"So you're a car thief? And you didn't get in any trouble? Why didn't he make you pay for the car?" I asked, genuinely curious.

"Because, to my father, the image of the perfect son was what he wanted. The car didn't fit with that image, so he made it disappear. I wish my father had made me pay for it or had me experience some sort of punishment, but he didn't. He used his money to make everything all better. It's the story of my life with him," he said. He seemed surprised at his own words. His eyes lifted back up, piercing into me. "Your turn."

I thought for a moment. "It's no stealing a car, but it's something I don't tell anyone. Ever." I frowned. This wasn't something I enjoyed telling people. I knew I could tell Jack though. It was like we had no secrets between us and I could tell him anything without fear. I knew instinctively that he would never laugh at me or judge me the way everyone else in my life did. There was a sense of safety I had never felt with anyone else that made me want to tell him everything about me. "I was bulimic in high school. Everyone thought I looked great, and it was so hard to stop when I finally had people asking if I had lost weight."

"Why did you stop?"

"My dad is a dentist. He saw the acid damage on my teeth and told my mom. They never looked at me quite the same again after that," I said, my voice cracking. I tried to hide it with a sip of water. "I still struggle with it, you know? My mom and sister are these perfect thin stick people, and I'm not. I don't like the way I look. I don't like the way my clothes fit, but no matter what I do, it isn't enough. I know that people look at me and the extra weight is all they see. I lost boyfriend because of it. He said he didn't want to be with a 'fat chick'. I am terrified that I am going to end up alone because of it." I was shaking a little by the time I stopped talking.

"I don't see how that is possible. Your boyfriend was an idiot. You are beautiful," Jack said, his eyes catching mine. He made sure I could see the truth in them as he continued. "I would date you if I met you in real life." His face held a heat that made my insides start to tingle. My heart skipped a beat and I could feel my knees spread under the table. He thought I was beautiful.

"Don't say it if you don't mean it."

"I mean every word."

"No one has ever called me beautiful. Other than my dad, but that doesn't count."

"Then they are all idiots. Except your dad, because you are beautiful."

His eyes glowed caramel in the candlelight, full of honest appreciation. The heat in his eyes told me that he found me more than beautiful.

"What are you afraid of?" I asked quickly, changing the subject. The blush on my cheeks was threatening to light the table on fire.

"Spiders," he answered nonchalantly.

"Spiders. That doesn't count," I said, giggling. He smiled at me and shrugged as though he were trying to take off an invisible weight.

"I'm afraid I will end up alone, but in a different way. I don't have any real friends, at least none outside my work. I'm so busy with my job that I don't have time to make connections and the ones I do make are tainted by business. I feel like life is passing me by. I'm surrounded by people, but I hardly know any of them and I feel like I can't get to know them." He peered into his water glass, sliding the liquid back and forth. "I'm afraid I'm going to miss days like today."

His hand reached out and touched mine. A spark of desire, want, and need jumped between us. I was sure the tablecloth was going to explode with the current passing between us. He leaned forward, his perfect lips coming closer. I leaned closer, wanting to taste them. The table grew smaller.

At that moment the waitress returned with our meals. The spell we had woven with our secrets was broken. Jack ordered some wine and we settled into our food, our conversation drifting back to mundane topics. We still laughed and conversed easily, but the magic of secret sharing was lost.

We ordered dessert and I was surprised by how easily our conversation continued to flow. I could feel the wine making me laugh more than usual, but it had never been this easy to talk to a guy... ever,... even with much more alcohol than a bottle of wine. I found my hand drifting towards his on multiple occasions, but I kept my fingers to myself. I wanted to touch him and make sure he was real, but I didn't want to scare him away. I wanted to do so much more than just touch him.

The waitress came and refilled our wine glasses several times, but I barely noticed. The wine was delicious, but I couldn't take my eyes off Jack — the way the candle lit up his eyes, the way he brushed his hand through his hair when he was thinking, the way he looked at me, and how I found myself telling him things I had never told another living soul. Before I knew it, we were the only ones left in the restaurant.

"Would you like to come back to my place?" I blurted out, the wine making me bold. I held in a nervous giggle, but I was sure I looked ridiculous. I certainly felt ridiculous; there was no way a man as handsome, charming, and wealthy as Jack would ever come back with me to my room. Things like that don't happen to me. Men don't look at me like that.

"I thought you would never ask," he said with a pleased smile. I couldn't believe my luck. I stood up slowly and tucked the chair neatly into the table. Jack offered me his elbow, and together we sauntered out of the restaurant and back towards the beach.

We walked up the beach, the moon shining down like a giant spotlight. White tipped waves shushed the darkness as we approached. I had never seen so many stars in the sky; they seemed to go on forever. I wished the walk was longer so I could hold on to the moment and keep it in my mind forever. Everything was perfect. The ocean was perfect. The man holding my arm like a gentleman was perfect. The evening had been perfect and I was terrified that it was all going to end the moment I stepped on my porch.

ࡄࡘ ࡘࡄ

CHAPTER FOUR

The porch creaked slightly as I stepped up and unlocked the door. I could feel him move in behind me, resting his weight on an arm against the door frame. I turned slowly, captured against the door and his body. His masculine scent made my knees feel weak, and my throat felt dry as he leaned over me, his eyes searching mine. His expression was intense, almost threatening; I looked up into those hazel eyes, the moonlight making them shine with something I wanted. *Desire. He wanted me.* The thought alone made me shiver with anticipation, as he brought his hand to my neck and pulled my lips towards his.

His mouth was hot against mine, his tongue probing gently at my lips, asking to taste me. I opened my mouth and he shifted his weight to kiss me fully. He explored me in a slow and thorough manner before pulling back. His eyes gleamed with an aching hunger that held me captive. I wanted him more than anything.

He pushed me back until I bumped against the door. His mouth skimmed my jaw, down to my throat, his teeth grazing my skin and his five-o-clock shadow scratching gently. He pressed a thigh between my legs, sending heat through my belly and then south. I whimpered for more, the noise low in my throat.

"You want to invite me in?" he whispered in my ear. Goosebumps ran down my arms, but not from cold.

"Why? Are you a vampire?" I asked with a wry smile.

He didn't answer but instead kissed me again, drawing me to him like a magnet. He wrapped his arms around me and pulled on my waist, guiding me through the open door. He released me and I felt woozy on my feet from his kisses. The door thudded softly shut and I licked my lips.

He was perfect in the moonlight. His shoulders were broad, tapering into a tight waist and an ass that my fingers itched to squeeze. The darkness and the wine made me bold, my desire growing by the minute. His eyes caught mine and he smiled, knowing that I was checking him out. Those eyes turned up the flame growing in my belly, now spreading north and south, filling my core with need. The sexual tension wrapped around us like taut guitar strings, filling the room with vibrating desire.

His hands grabbed my hips again, pulling me into

him with strong fingers. I wrapped my arms around his shoulders, tangling my fingers in his hair as we stumbled towards the bedroom. A part of me told me that I should stop, that I should think this through, but the other voices in my head quickly drowned her out; I wanted him more than I wanted to breathe.

Before we got to the bed, he ran his fingertips up my sides, his touches reading the curves of my body. His eyes were locked with mine, and the smoldering flame within them silenced even that last voice that resisted him. We held this position, and the intensity of the moment made it stretch out for what seemed like an eternity. Then, as if on cue, we both went in for another kiss.

As our tongues locked, I felt my body surrender to him. I wanted him, and I would do anything to have him. I felt like we were on our own little island, marooned in our own little shack, and nothing else that went on around us mattered. His hands went back down to my hips, and his fingers began to pull upward, bunching my sundress up. With every stroke of his finger against my hip, I felt shivers up my spine. His hands shifted further behind me, and as the bottom of my dress reached his fingers, I felt him lightly touch my ass.

My own hands went to his chest, his white t-shirt the only thing between me and those solid pectorals of his. I pulled at the shirt, and as his arms flew upward I could feel the hem of my dress fall back down. I sheepishly laughed, but as he threw his shirt on the floor, I got my first look at that muscular chest of his. My hands went to it, my palms rubbing against the muscles, feeling him. I came back in for another kiss.

In a moment, I found myself lifted up, and I squealed in delight. His hands had found their way back to my bottom, and like a caveman, he threw me over his shoulder. I had never had a man do this to me, and I lightly slapped his back, as if I could offer any resistance at this point. In another moment, I found myself falling towards the bed where I wanted to be.

He stood over me as I lay on the bed, knees bent, my dress hiking up towards my thighs. He took a foot in his hand, kissing it gingerly. Immediately, I felt self-conscious. What if he noticed how big my feet were? I drew back, but with a firm grasp, he yanked my foot back, going back to his tender kisses. As soon as he pulled, he had let me know who was in charge now, and I surrendered.

His kisses moved up my calf, bringing me closer to the edge of the bed, closer to the edge of bliss. I knew his destination, so I closed my eyes and let it happen. I felt his kisses move up, slowly, deliberately, driving me crazy.

He fell to his knees as my ass moved to the edge of the bed. I felt him hike my skirt up and I spread my legs to let him get where he wanted. I felt his fingers wrap around the edges of the bikini bottom I had left on under my dress. With the deftness of a locksmith, he slid them down off my hips, exposing me to his eyes.

A thousand thoughts were going through my head. What would he think? Am I neat and tidy down there? Are my thighs rubbing together? Those thoughts faded to nothingness as his tongue went to flower, tasting me gingerly. The only thought that went through my head was that I wanted more, and in a moment he delivered. His tongue flicked against me with the tempo and pressure of a practiced lover.

Soon I felt my hands going to my breasts through my dress. As I touched them, I thought of the ocean right outside the walls of this cabana. His pace never wavered, and I could feel a swell forming on the horizon. My hands went to his hair, trying to pull him in, trying to get *more*. The swell grew and grew, and soon my entire body was heaving. I squeezed my eyes shut as the tidal wave crashed onto my shores, sweeping all my cares and worries away.

I felt my legs squeeze on Jack's head and willed them to separate, but he never stopped his tongue's movement. A few moments later, the sensation became too intense. My legs squeezed shut again and I grabbed Jack's hair and pulled him up. He smiled a devilish grin at me before grabbing the bottom of my dress and lifting. I sat up, and as his fingers moved past my breasts, he lifted my bikini top up with my dress. In another moment, I was naked, exposed to judgment by this Adonis.

And judge me he did. I could hear him growl appreciatively as he appraised my body. My breasts were full and the nipples were even harder with the sudden cool air hitting them.

I watched as he pulled his shorts down, revealing his manhood. It was already completely erect, and my eyes popped out a little at how big he was. I laughed to myself when I thought of what his secretary was missing out on.

He rummaged in the pockets of his bathing suit while it was in his hands, pulling out a cell phone and a wallet. He carefully placed his phone on the nightstand next to the bed before opening his wallet and pulling out a square package. I smiled. He *was* thoughtful.

He tore the package open, pulling out the condom inside. I watched as he rolled the condom over his member. This was all happening so fast, I didn't know what to think, I didn't know if I should stop him or if I should go with it.

He leaned down, whispering in my ear. "What's your favorite position?"

No man had ever asked me that. Vacation me decided to go with it. "The one we're in right now is just fine," I said with a quick giggle.

"Then I'll start right here," he said, breathing into my ear. As his thick member rubbed against my opening, I felt him hold his breath, and I held mine. I wanted it as bad as he did, and it showed, because he slid right into me. Both of us gasped, then his lips were on mine in an instant. As he moved against my body, I felt rapturous. I kissed him with more passion than I had ever kissed a man in my life.

He leaned up, propping himself up on his hands as he thrust into me. My hands moved to his biceps, strong and large as he supported his weight. My fingers kneaded at his muscles as he filled me with his throbbing manhood.

He pulled out of me and lay next to me on his

side. His hand grabbed my shoulder, pushing me onto my side as well, facing away from him. As he spooned me, his fingernails drifted down my side, ending up at my hip. The light sensation made me shiver with anticipation as he pushed himself between my legs. I opened to him, and he immediately began breathing in my ear, his ragged breaths telling me just how much he wanted me. I began to move against him, our bodies undulating together in a harmony that I had never felt before. His hand grabbed my hips and held on tight, moving me the way that he wanted me to move. I liked having him in control.

He leaned back and thrust harder, then pulled out. He rolled onto his back and lay there, letting me drink in the sight of him. We waited there for a moment, and I didn't know what to do. He gave a mischievous grin and beckoned to me with a finger. I felt a blush creep across my cheeks as I realized he was letting me be on top. I got up on my knees and mounted him, and he smiled as I moved down on him.

I writhed against him, and he eyed my body hungrily. I pressed my arms together, knowing it would make my average breasts look even fuller for him. He looked my entire body up and down, and as I began to writhe faster, his fingers again traced their way up my back. I had never felt fuller than I did right then.

With a sudden motion, he grabbed my hair in his right hand and clenched. I gasped, and his powerful left hand brought my body against his. Despite me being on top, he was very much in charge. As his right hand grabbed more of my hair, he guided my motions. He held me against him, every square inch of our bodies touching. His right hand pulled upward and I began to moan, the pain spiking the pleasure with every thrust. His left hand moved down to my ass, kneading at the fleshy cheek, spreading me open even further. My moans became more and more frantic, and I could feel sweat dripping down my body.

His mouth went to my ear and I could hear his ragged breathing as he exerted himself. "You're incredible," he said, and the way he said it was enough to drive me wild. He was in control, my body responding to his every motion. He began to pound into me, and within another moment he rolled me on my side. He kept going, still inside of me, until he was on top and I was on bottom.

We were back to a missionary position, but it was anything but boring. There was a wild need in his eyes as he continued to make love to me. A look of primal, almost animal lust. He craved release, and so did I. I reached my hands around to his perfect ass, pulling him in as if I could bring him even closer to me. His eyes scanned my entire body, and every inch of my body seemed to be turning him on. The ache in the pit of my stomach was almost too much to bare, and as I felt the sweat drip from his body onto mine, I knew that this was it.

He got a strained look in his eyes, and I couldn't help but cry out, digging my fingers into his arm as he pushed into me, again and again. With his first primal grunt, I felt my body burst in a blissful explosion that threatened to tear me apart. I heard another animal groan, and another as his thrusts went deep.

In another moment, he collapsed onto me, our sweaty bodies sliding all over each other. He pulled out of me, quickly removing the condom and throwing it towards the trash bin. He missed and hit the floor next to it. He made no move to retrieve it. I sighed as I looked at the muscular man who was now lying back next to me. Nobody's perfect, but nothing would ruin this perfect moment.

I don't know when I fell asleep, but I know I was in his arms, listening to his heartbeat. I was sure I was going to wake up and have this all just be a wonderful dream, but even if it was, it was a dream I would never forget.

CHAPTER FIVE

ఇండ్ర ఏండ

The sun shone directly into my eyes, waking me from a dead sleep. With a groan, I threw my arm over my face, rolling into my pillow. It smelled like Jack, masculine and intoxicating. I moved my arm and could feel the cool linen next to me; Jack was long gone from my bed. I kept my face buried in the pillow, my eyes shut tight. Maybe if I didn't open them, I wouldn't have to wake up and find him truly gone.

My bladder, however, had a different idea. I lay still trying to convince myself to go back to sleep, but I finally couldn't fight it any longer. I stood up and let the sheets fall from my naked body as I hurried to the bathroom, the tile cold on my bare feet.

The face in the mirror watched me as I washed my hands and ran a brush through my hair, trying to coax the tangles into some sort of pony tail. I felt pleasantly sore all over, and the memory of the night before made me smile before I realized he had left without even waking me.

"Of course he left. He saw me in the morning light, drooling in my sleep, and escaped as quickly as possible. Good thing I wasn't lying on his arm or he would have had to chew it off," I mumbled to myself as I threw on a sundress and headed outside.

He was gone, but the whole evening was so worth it. It had seemed almost magical, and while I was sad that it was over, I knew it was a memory that would last forever.

I stepped out on the porch, ready to go get breakfast by myself when I saw him. He was sitting on my porch, his long legs stretched out and crossed at the ankles as he sat reading in the shade. I blinked twice, sure he was not really there. A man that attractive and that good in bed was not going to hang around me too long.

"Good morning, Sleepy-head. I thought you were going to sleep the day away," he said setting the book down. His smile was even better in the morning light.

"You're still here," I said stumbling over the words. "I woke up and thought you had left."

"After a showing like last night? I may never leave," he replied with a mischievous grin. I bit my lip and grinned at him.

"It was pretty good, wasn't it," I said. He stood up and crossed the porch in a single step, his arms wrapping around me like they had always been there.

"Better than good," he whispered before leaning forward to kiss me. I felt the heat rise inside of me again, and I was about to drag him back into the bedroom when his pocket began ringing loudly. He sighed and let me go, stepping back reluctantly to answer his phone.

"What is it?" Jack said harshly into the phone. His voice was full of power, but none of the sensuality from the night before. I stepped down and sat on the porch step, pushing my feet out of the shade of the porch and into the sun. Jack growled into the phone and leaned against the far railing. My feet played in the hot sand as I waited for him to finish his call, trying my best not to listen in on his conversation. Instead, I stared out at the endless ocean. The sky was a bright blue that merged almost seamlessly with the dark water in the distance. It was going to be another perfect day in paradise.

"Emma," Jack said sitting down next to me. I liked the way my name sounded when he said it. "I have to leave for a little bit. There is something I have to take care of that can't wait. Business."

"I understand," I tried to sound like it didn't matter. My voice cracked, betraying me. I had been in this spot before; he wanted to get away while he still could. He pushed a tendril of hair behind my ear and turned my face to look at him. His expression was soft, but his eyes told me he was in complete control and he knew it.

"I will meet you here in two hours. Don't be late," he said right before he kissed me. I knew it was a goodbye kiss. I hoped it was only goodbye for two hours and not forever.

***

I watched him hurry off down the beach, talking forcefully into his phone, and then he slowly disappeared. My heart ached to see him go. I didn't know what scared me more, the idea that he was never coming back, or that he would be back in two hours. Jack evoked such a range of emotions that I felt confused by them all. I searched the horizon for a single stationary object to help me keep my emotional balance, but found nothing. I wanted him to come back, but I was scared of what it meant if he did. The level of attraction I felt towards him wasn't something I was ready for. This was only a vacation after all, and I was going to have to say goodbye to him eventually. I didn't want to think about it.

I ate a small breakfast at the resort cafe and then hurried back to our spot on the beach. The tide was going out, so I passed the time looking for shells and shiny rocks. It was such a simple thing to do, but I found myself chasing the waves, trying to catch small stones and pieces of drift wood before the ocean could reclaim them. I giggled, feeling like a wonder-filled child, as I found a small shell and released it onto a wave, watching it drift away. I looked at my watch. It had been a little over the two hours, and I looked around full of hope. My hope quickly turned to an emptiness as I looked up and down the beach and couldn't find him. My little floating shell had sunk quickly in the waves and I didn't want to play anymore.

I bit my lip, ashamed that tears were forming along

the edges of my eyes. I squeezed my eyes shut as hard as I could and took a deep breath. Last night had been amazing and I would always have that. Jack was obviously a busy man, and this was only a vacation after all. This wasn't real life.

"Sorry I'm late," a deep voice said behind me. I turned to see Jack wading into the water, the cuffs of his shorts already damp from the waves. He smiled and my heart pounded like a drum in my chest. He came back. He had come back... for me.

"I was beginning to think you weren't coming," I said quietly. I tried to keep the hurt out of my voice. He looked at his hands and I realized he was breathing hard. He must have run the whole way here.

"Sometimes I hate my job. Even on vacation, I don't really get a day off. I apologize for making you wait," he replied somberly. His eyes shone with honesty as he reached my spot in the water. "What are you doing out here?"

"Chasing the waves," I said. I had completely forgiven him. When he looked at me like that, I think I would have forgiven anything. "What would you like to do?"

He smiled and kissed me softly. My hands pressed against his strong chest as the water swirled around our knees. "Walk with me?"

He grabbed my hand and led me out of the water. My skirt clung to my wet legs as we walked along the beach. His hand felt strong in mine, like he would never let me go again. I wished that he didn't have to, that we could stay in this sunshine filled moment forever. We walked for a while, the sand feeling good under my feet. There were some locals in tents along the beach hocking their trinkets, bobbles sand treasures. Each tent held gems, jewelry, liquor and paintings in all shapes and sizes.

"A pretty necklace for a pretty lady?" A strongly accented local called out as we walked past a blue tent. He was another in a long line of tents strung along the beach. I giggled and kept walking as the merchants called out their wares to us.

We stopped several times to look at the beautiful things for sale, but I never saw anything that I wanted until the last shop in the row. It was a simple silver pendant in the shape of a dolphin, but something about it called to me. I hadn't seen another like it in any of the shops. Jack smiled as he saw me pick it up and admire it.

"The lady has excellent taste," the shop keeper cooed as he saw me pick it up. "Put it on. See how it feels."

Jack took the delicate chain from my fingers and deftly placed it around my neck. The dolphin fit perfectly in the hollow of my throat. Jack stepped back and smiled.

"How much for the necklace?" he asked the shop keeper. The old man frowned and looked at the necklace before answering.

"$100 American dollars. But for you, I sell it at $85," he smiled, his teeth bright.

"$85? That is too much. Thank you though. It is beautiful," I said quickly. I reached up to undo the clasp and return it to the jewelry tray. I knew that I could negotiate him down, but I had to act like I was going to leave it.

"No. The lady will have it," Jack interjected, placing his hand on the back of my neck so I couldn't reach the clasp.

"What are you doing? It isn't worth that," I hissed at him. He ignored me and fished money out of his wallet and handed it to the man.

"Thank you, sir. Enjoy the necklace, miss," the shop keep said with a grin as he counted the money greedily. I shook my head slowly, but I the proud smile on Jack's face kept my mouth shut. If I didn't know for sure he was rich before, I certainly knew it now.

We stepped out of the merchant's stall and were immediately swarmed by the neighboring tents' merchants. Every single one of them called out in sweet voices, trying to coax us like sirens to their wares. Every stall we passed had a salesman trying to pull us into their shop. One physically grabbed my arm to pull me under his tent to look at his jewelry, making me squeak and stumble away. Jack's face twisted as though he tasted something sour, and he grabbed my hand and pulled me to the water. The merchants still kept hawking their wares, but at least they couldn't pluck at our clothing. We walked through the waves, still following the white sandy line of the ocean. I secretly hoped we would walk around the entire island instead of turning around.

"I buy one thing and they all go crazy," he said, looking back at the tents like they might follow us out into the ocean.

"That's because you paid full price," I said with a giggle. He looked at me and furrowed his brows. "I willingly admit that I am not the best haggler, but I could have gotten him down to at least $30. You flashed your money and now they know you don't haggle."

"Oh, come on, $85 isn't that much! It isn't something to justify the feeding frenzy of salesmen. Now I know how chum feels when the sharks gather." He glanced back over his shoulder like they still might be chasing us.

"$85 is a lot of money to spend on a necklace, no matter how pretty it is." I couldn't help but smile at the look on his face, his head tilted slightly as though I had said the sky was made of chocolate.

"It isn't that much," he said. If I didn't know better, I would have said a pout crossed his handsome mouth.

"It is to them. It certainly is to me. $85 is almost a full day's pay." I shrugged like it was nothing, but he stopped walking and dropped my hand in surprise. I fiddled with the silver charm, sliding it up and down on its simple chain. I hadn't meant to bring up how different our economic situations were. He stayed quiet for a moment and then cleared his throat. I had a horrible feeling that he was thinking of bolting. "Thank you for the necklace though. I really do like it, even if it is a little extravagant."

Jack's face relaxed and he smiled at me. His shoulders dropped from his ears and he reached out a hand to me again.

"You deserve even more. The charm suits you. I

like it on you," he said waiting for me to take his hand. I played with the cool silver charm in my fingers for a moment before grinning at him.

"It does look good, doesn't it?" I reached for his hand. A spark of energy flowed through his fingers into mine. It made my heart speed up and my stomach do happy flips. He smiled and squeezed my hand and we continued down the beach and away from the shops. I felt like a princess wearing something sparkly, hand in hand with her knight in shining armor. A girl could get used to extravagance.

CHAPTER SIX

The afternoon sun shone down on the two of us and we walked alongside the waves and giggled at stupid jokes. I felt more comfortable with him than I had with anyone in my life. He seemed to relax the longer we walked. I wished I could have more days like this, but both our vacations were going to have to end soon. I pushed the thought as far from my mind as I could.

"What's the craziest thing you've ever done?" Jack asked as I bent down to pick up a seashell. I studied the shell for a moment before casting it out into the ocean.

"You are going to make fun of me," I said, squinting out at the horizon before looking at him. He grinned mischievously.

"I'm going to make more fun of you if you don't tell me," he said, his eyes sparkling. I glared at him before answering.

"I went skinny dipping in Old Man Smith's fishing pond. A bunch of us did it one night," I said finally, a blush creeping into my cheeks.

"That doesn't sound that crazy," he scoffed gently.

"Well, it wasn't... until he came out with a shotgun and threatened to shoot us all for scaring his fish," I giggled. "I nearly ran the whole way home before I realized I was naked and had forgotten my clothes by the pond. To top it off, my parents had dinner guests that night. I had to sneak in, naked, past three different sets of dentists."

"Did any of them see you?" he asked, his sides quivering as he tried not to laugh.

"I hid in the garage until I found a winter coat. One of the guests saw me and gave me this weird look as I dashed up the stairs with bare legs and a heavy overcoat, but I made it," I said shaking my head and laughing at the memory. Jack let his laughter mix with mine as he teased me about forgetting my clothes as we walked hand in hand down the beach.

Up ahead, white gauze streamers caught my attention. Jack followed my gaze to the small arbor decorated with pretty white fabric and tropical flowers. A bored looking attendant in a white dress shirt and pants sat next to it playing on his phone.

"You ever think you'll get married?" Jack asked nodding towards the awning.

"At the rate I'm going? No. You don't even want to know the last time I went on a date. I want to, but, no one seems interested. I've kind of come to accept that I will be a crazy old cat lady someday." The admission hurt, but it was freeing to say it out loud. Jack squeezed my hand. "What about you? You think you'll ever marry?" I asked him as we approached the small wedding area. The attendant fanned himself with a brochure packet as he slid his phone into the pocket of his shirt and watched us disinterestedly.

"Honestly, I don't know. I would love a family. I want a wife and kids with a dog in a white picket fenced yard, but I don't think that will ever happen because of my work and the obligations that come with it. The fact that I have money complicates things. If I were to get married, it would have to be to someone who could see past my job and the income. Someone who wanted to be with *me*," he said it like it didn't bother him, but the edges of his voice held a deep pain. I wondered who had hurt him over money to make him so distrustful.

"I'd marry you. Even if you didn't have any money," I blurted out. He stopped and looked at me, his eyes dark. I bit my lip and looked up at him. "I mean, I don't know how much money you have, but I know that I like being around you. I think I like you more than anyone I have ever met."

Jack pulled me so I was facing him. I could feel the blush on my cheeks increasing as he searched my face.

"You're serious," he said slowly, a smile blossoming on his face. I nodded and blushed harder. "You want to get married?" he asked, tipping his head towards the white arbor.

"Sure, why not?" I answered with a smile. I wasn't about to back out of this conversation now. I already said I would marry him and I wasn't going to miss this opportunity to tease him later when he was the one who backed out.

"Let's do it then," he said with a wicked smile. I felt my mouth open and I couldn't quite close it; he wasn't supposed to take me seriously.

"Are you serious?"

"Sure, why not?" he mimicked me with a grin. He pulled me by the hand towards the awning like he was very serious.

"Wait a second," I gasped.

"Oh, so you're backing out?" Jack's eyes twinkled with amusement.

"No, I am not backing out. I said I would marry you and I will," I responded feeling full of sass. "I want to... ummm... clarify a couple of things."

"Okay, Ms. Worrywart, go on — clarify," he said with a laugh.

"It is soon to be Mrs. Worrywort. You realize that we are in a foreign country right?" I asked. He nodded and I felt a surge of relief that I hoped would be enough to satisfy the rational part of my brain. We were both foreign here and didn't have the right paperwork, so this would never be considered legal. There would be no consequence for this. A giddy surge of excitement went through me. This was what an adventure was supposed to feel like. "Good. You realize that you never asked my dad's permission?"

"You want me to call him right now?" Jack asked innocently as he began reaching for his phone. "Or are you just thinking up excuses not to marry me?"

I laughed and pushed his hand away from his

pocket. There was no way I was going to let him win this game. "Oh, I'll marry the hell out of you. Besides, then we can tell everyone we are on our honeymoon and get free drinks."

"You are staying on an all-inclusive resort," he snorted and I pushed him playfully.

"Before we do this though, you should at least propose properly," I said trying to keep a straight face. Jack looked thoughtful for a moment before taking my hand and dropping to one knee.

"My dearest, loveliest Emma," he began looking up at me with his hazel eyes full of laughter. I couldn't have wiped the goofy smile off my face if he had paid me. "Will you do me the biggest honor of this vacation, and marry me?"

"Yes," I giggled. He stood up and kissed me. He kissed me back with a passion I wasn't expecting. It was like the wind was sucked out of my lungs and replaced with desire. He pulled away slowly after a moment, our eyes connecting. My breath came in small gasps.

"Come on!" Jack recovered first and grabbed my hand with a smile, pulling me towards the pretty awning. I nearly tripped over my own feet, but I wasn't about to be late for my own wedding.

***

"I now pronounce you husband and wife," the man in the white shirt said in a thick accent. I barely understood any of the words he said during the ceremony, simply repeating "I do" whenever he paused. "You may now kiss the bride."

Jack smiled at me. I would have married him ten times over for that smile. My insides felt mushy and happy in a way I couldn't describe or understand, but when he kissed me, everything felt perfect. His lips were soft against mine, his tongue slipping in at the last second. This is what a vacation should feel like, I thought to myself. I was truly having an adventure. No one at home would ever believe that I had married a stranger, let alone one as handsome as Jack. This was something that I would treasure forever.

"Smile for the camera," the minister said holding up a digital camera. Jack's hand went up and covered the lens before he could snap a picture.

"No pictures," he growled at the man. The minister paled slightly but then smiled as he glanced back and forth between us.

"No pictures?" I asked, turning towards Jack. "Not even one, just for us?"

Jack frowned for a moment, then lowered his hand and reached in his pocket. "No pictures except this one. This one is for us," he said as he pulled out his phone and handed it to the minister. Jack and I posed under the white awning, looking for all the world like newlyweds as the camera phone clicked.

The minister nodded happily as he handed back the phone to Jack. Jack grinned as he saw the screen and handed it to me. I gasped. I looked beautiful. Jack looked so handsome and we both looked genuinely happy. If I didn't know better, I would have thought this was an actual wedding photo.

"I better get a copy," I said as I handed him his

phone. Jack laughed, and caught me up in his arms, pulling me in for another kiss. My head spun as he kissed me and nipped gently at my bottom lip with his teeth. I lost myself in his kiss.

"You'll get the only copy," he whispered. "This is ours and ours alone. No one can ever take this from us. This is our secret, one only we share." His breath tickled my ear and made a heat surge between my thighs. I wondered how he could make my body react so quickly without even trying. His chest was strong beneath me and I could feel something hardening against my hip. I couldn't wait to get him back to the hotel room.

"We should head back and start our honeymoon," I whispered, pushing my hips against his. His hand tightened on my back and I wished I could have him right there on the sand.

"Ahem," the man who married us coughed and raised his eyebrows. I felt the blush surge back onto my cheeks as Jack released me. I wondered if the minister could feel the energy between us, but he rolled his eyes and waited for us to leave his awning.

Jack grabbed my hand, his fingers entwining with mine. I wanted our legs to entwine like that, and together we hurried along the beach to begin our time as man and wife.

CHAPTER SEVEN

I could hear him snoring gently in the bedroom through the open window. His breathing was slow and even, the soft rumbles of his sleep soothing. I sat with my feet curled up under me on the wicker porch chair looking out at the rolling waves and listening to my husband sleep.

I found myself smiling. I had this wonderful serene sense of calm and perfection. I could get used to this marriage thing. The world finally felt perfect. I knew it was all a lie, that in two days I would leave the ocean and this marriage would just be another page in my scrapbook, but today, I didn't care. Today was perfect.

Last night had been amazing. Yesterday had been amazing. I still couldn't believe I was a married woman, if only for a little bit. Jack had taken me back to my cabana and showed me what a husband should do for his wife. Thinking about the pleasure his hands and tongue could create made my temperature rise.

This sense of happiness held a danger though. I was falling for him — falling for him hard. He was wonderful, sexy, and could make me laugh. He was my perfect man,... and I was going to have to leave him forever in three days. I wanted more of him and I had a sinking feeling that I always would. This love was like our marriage—a happy illusion.

A gull flew overhead, squawking loudly about a lost supper as he searched for more. The ocean was almost green today with clouds blocking the brightness of the sun. The sky threatened rain in the evening, but for now, the world was hot and sticky. It made everything more dreamlike. I closed my eyes and listened to ocean, feeling the warm breeze glide across my skin and ruffle my sundress.

The front door creaked and I kept my eyes shut, lost in my happy moment. "Good morning."

"Good morning to you too, sleepy head," I said with a grin. I opened my eyes and wanted to gasp. Jack stood admiring the view, and I couldn't help but admire mine. He stood wearing only a pair of blue swim trunks, bare-chested and hair still rumpled from sleep. He stretched and my eyes followed the play of muscles down his chest and abs, feeling my insides go mushy.

"I haven't slept like that in years." Jack ran a hand through his perfect bedhead hair. I wanted to put my fingers in it again, to pull his face close to mine and kiss him thoroughly. "What did you do to me?"

"Just my wifely duties," I said, stretching my legs out from under me. Jack's eyes followed my legs with obvious interest. His hand dropped from his sandy hair and he grinned as his eyes met mine. I stood up slowly, feeling stiff. I was sore all over, but in a good way. My body had never seen this much sex, let alone this much good sex. Muscles I didn't even know I had were letting me know I was using them. It was great.

"I thought I would go for a morning swim before breakfast. You interested?" The glimmer in his eye made me hope there was more than swimming. Those muscles needed more exercise.

"Breakfast was a couple of hours ago, Sleepy Head, but I'll join you for one before lunch," I quipped. I stood and rose to my toes, giving him a quick peck before turning to change into my swim suit

"Hold it right there, Beautiful," Jack growled catching my arm and pulling me back to him. He leaned down and pressed his soft lips against mine, flooding my brain with sensation and desire. When he finally released me from his kiss, I staggered to the door gasping for breath.

"How do you kiss so *good*?" I asked as I opened the door. He grinned cockily at me. I hurried in and found a dry suit, a bright pink bikini that I never thought I would actually wear. I had bought it because I loved the color, but today I felt like I could wear it. Jack would love it.

Jack whistled as I stepped out. He was off the steps in the sand, looking up as I came out on the porch. The bikini felt tiny and exposing, but the way it made Jack's eyes light up took away any self-consciousness that I had. Jack liked it and that was all that mattered.

Jack's hand felt warm in mine, his fingers grasping mine tightly as we headed towards the green waves. Jack walked into the water as though it wasn't there. He sloshed effortlessly through the waves, pulling me along behind him. The water was cool, but it felt good after the tropical heat.

Jack dived under the water, releasing my hand. I stood still, letting the waves bump against me in the waist high water as I waited patiently for him to surface. A moment passed, and then another, and he didn't surface. A thread of worry began to creep into my chest as I turned in the water, searching for him.

Something grabbed my ankle and pulled me under. I yelped and felt salt water pour into my open mouth as my head dipped beneath the surface. I scrambled to the surface, spitting out the salty water. Jack rose laughing, water sluicing off his muscles and catching the light as I wiped the water out of my eyes.

"Gotcha."

I turned in an instant and tackled him, my arms wrapping around his solid middle and throwing all my weight into his hips. This time I was the one prepared to go under and he wasn't. Jack came up spluttering and laughing as he pulled me close to him. He held me effortlessly against him, our faces just above the surface and almost touching as he knelt in the water.

"You trying to drown me?" His voice had a thrilling gruffness to it.

"You started it," I whispered. His fingers splayed

against my back, pushing my chest into his. He felt so solid and warm in the water. I wrapped my legs around him, feeling his excitement growing.

His mouth covered mine, his lips soft and wet with the ocean. The salt water flavored his kisses, giving him a new taste that I could never hope to get enough of. I licked my lips, tasting his salt water kisses. This is what heaven was like.

He pulled me closer, our skin pressing together so that not even a single drop of water could fit between us. He was so warm and strong, my insides melting with fresh want. I would have taken him right there. I would have let him fill me and let my body sing his praise, but an old married couple was walking down the beach.

I bit my lip as I watched them walk slowly past us, and Jack made a deep masculine noise of appreciation before kissing the offended lip. "I think we should head back in and rinse off before lunch, what do you think?"

I arched my hips into his, feeling a growing hardness that made my body ache with desire. I nodded and grinned as I unhooked my legs and stood. He stood behind me, using me as his shield against the eyes of the beach walking couple once we reached shallow water.

We scurried across the sand back to our little cottage. As we got close to the front steps, he lunged ahead, grabbing my hand and pulling in. He didn't stop at the front door, or a the bedroom, but kept pulling me in until the shower. Jack turned on the water, grinning as he turned to face me.

The room quickly filled with mist from the hot water, swirling around us and fogging the mirror. Jack stepped closer, reaching up to untie the string of my top. His fingers were so gentle, so light, that all I could feel was the string give way and the wet swim suit sag. His pupils dilated and then focused as I reached behind me and undid the bottom string, the top falling off my body.

Jack licked his lips in an unconscious gesture of desire, before sliding one finger along my collar bone. It was so gentle, it felt more like a soft breeze, but my nipples beaded and begged to be touched. A male sound of appreciation escaped Jack, and he slowly glided his finger down the swell of my breast. I gasped as he pinched the nipple softly, sending just enough pain but far more pleasure through my system.

Jack dipped his head down, sliding his lips along my temple and down to my throat. His hands explored my exposed skin, sending shivers of delight as he caressed. His strong hands cupped my breasts, playing with their weight as he kissed the curve of my neck. His pecs were strong and warm beneath my hands, his skin smooth as I felt his chest.

Jack's hands slid down to my hips, his fingers picking up the wet fabric of my bikini bottoms before sliding them down my legs. He went to his knees as he pulled the fabric off, kissing my bellybutton as he ran his hands up and down my legs.

He sat back on his knees, admiring the view. I felt a blush creep over my cheeks and I covered breasts with my arm. Jack grabbed my hand, exposing me to him.

"God, you are beautiful."

He leaned forward and kissed my belly, his hands warm on my hips. His kisses were soft and gentle, like heavenly butterfly wings against my skin. A hand left my hip, tracing the line where my leg met my body until he came to the front. Jack looked up, his eyes bright and shining with desire as he dragged his finger along the line down my middle.

A deep noise of male appreciation escaped from him as he found I was ready for him. He grinned up at me, watching my reaction as he slowly traced a finger over me, teasing me with what he could do.

"Please," I gasped, every nerve on fire with want. He kissed my stomach again and slid between my folds, searching for my center. I moaned as he entered, gliding a second finger with the first and finding a sensual rhythm. His thumb moved to my pleasure center, rubbing slow circles as he rocked his hand in and out.

My body tightened as excitement thrummed through my veins. I could feel my temperature rising, the need for release building with every thrust of his fingers. I looked down to see only Jack's eyes. They shone with a desire to please, a love that had not yet been spoken. My body came, releasing the tension in a wave of pleasure that made me cry out. My vision blurred and for a moment I couldn't tell which direction was up or down.

I was still shuddering, lost in bliss as I heard the condom wrapper open. In the space of a breath he was before me, hard and thick between my legs. I spread my legs and he pushed inside, joining the two of us into one.

My back arched and I felt a second wave of pleasure course through me, my body tightening down on his. When the aching joy finally slowed enough to allow me to open my eyes, all I could see was the warm brown of Jack's. They were dark and fierce and filled with a need I wanted to satisfy.

He moved within me, pushing me back against the marble sink. It was a welcome cold compared to the steam filling the bathroom. I wrapped my legs around him, drawing him further into me as he grabbed the sink for leverage. Echoes of gasps and groans reverberated off the tile walls as his speed increased.

My spine felt like fire, our body heat combining with the steam to make everything slick. Jack's strokes were strong and sure, sending me into a happy oblivion. His breath was ragged in my ear, his need about to consume him. I felt him suddenly shudder, his body tightening and relaxing at the same time as he found release. My hips rocked hard into him, both of us gasping for breath before crumpling to the floor.

Our legs tangled together, arms wrapped in circles around one another. Jack drew back, still panting with exertion as he brushed a strand of hair behind my ear. His smile lit up my world, his body trembling and strong against mine.

I wanted to tell him I loved him. I wanted to tell him that he made my heart flutter and my body sing, but I couldn't find the courage. It wasn't fair to tell him, knowing that we could never be together. Big city and middle of nowhere don't go together for long.

"I think the water is ready," he murmured, his voice husky. The steam from the shower was nearly opaque at this point, but I didn't want to let him go yet. He made no move to untangle himself, our bodies still entwined on the cool tile floor. After a wonderful moment of eternity, we both loosened our limbs around the other.

Jack offered his hand, pulling me up easily from the floor. He didn't release it though, as he turned to the shower and stepped inside. I followed him into the spray of hot water and smiled. He hummed softly as he rinsed his hair, never releasing my hand. I stepped under the hot spray, letting it rinse the salt and sweat. The hot water coursed down the two of us as he leaned down and kissed me. His kiss still had a soft saltwater tang, and I smiled and leaned into him for more.

CHAPTER EIGHT

"Have you seen my black swimsuit?"

"You already packed it. It's in the front pouch of your suitcase."

"Thanks," I said with a flustered grin as I put the now dry pink suit in with the black one. Jack sat on the bed, watching me bounce around the bedroom picking things up and putting them in my suitcase. "When does your flight leave again?"

Jack sighed and shifted his weight on the foot of the bed. "It technically leaves whenever I am ready, but, I have to be back in New York by the close of business, so I need to leave in about fifteen minutes."

"I wish you didn't have to go until evening," I said quietly as I put the last couple of items in my main suitcase. What I really meant was, *I wish you didn't have to leave me at all.*

"Me too, but planes can only fly so fast," Jack

answered. He shifted his weight again.

"Anxious to be off?" I asked, nodding at his tapping toes. He couldn't seem to sit still. He looked down at his feet and saw his toes tapping against his sandals.

"It's a good thing I wear covered toe shoes at work," he murmured glaring at the offending foot. The toes stopped tapping. "I need to tell you something."

I played with the zipper on my suitcase for a moment before standing. I had a feeling something like this was going to happen. We had been far too happy, this vacation too perfect for it to not have some hidden secret. I had been watching him all morning and knew he was fighting with a decision. I could tell from the way his jaw clenched tight or the fact he ordered plain black coffee that he was nervous about something. We had only been together for less than a week, but I could read his subtle tells like I had known him my whole life.

"The secretary you came with... she's actually your wife, right?" I said straightening up to face him. I had been running scenarios of what he was going to say all morning. That was the most plausible one I could come up with. There were others, but asking him if he was a spy for the American government seemed a bit much.

Jack barked a short laugh. "No, not by a long-shot." His face darkened, and he stood up and took my hands in his. "I haven't been completely honest with you about what I do. I'm the new CEO of DS Oil and Gas."

I snorted. That was not one of the many scenarios I had concocted. "I knew you had money, Jack, but a billionaire? Be serious."

"I am serious. My father is the founder and owner of DS Oil and Gas. This is my last vacation before going back to take over the company. When my father steps down, I'll be in charge of the company." His eyes were dark and pleading. I could feel my brow furrowing as I shook my head and took my hands out of his.

"DS Oil and Gas? What are you talking about Jack?"

"I love that you don't know that. Here," he said pulling out his phone and pulling up a video. He placed it in my hands as the screen loaded. It was a commercial I had seen a thousand times, played on all the TV shows my parent's watched. The jingle was one of those stupid songs that had the instant ability to stay stuck in my head for days. *DS Oil and Gas... It's a blast!* On the last frame an attractive teenage boy came and stood by a distinguished older gentleman looking at an oil well. It was very obviously the teenage version of Jack with a man who could only be his father.

Jack gingerly took the phone from my shaking fingers when the video ended. "The video is a little old, but it's the one everyone knows. DS stands for Daniel Saunders, my father."

I looked up at him, confused. He reached out and gently pushed my chin closed; I hadn't realized it was hanging open. "I don't know what to say. I had no idea that was you."

"I think that's why I like you so much. You never saw me as a meal ticket or anything other than another human being. You didn't see a billionaire playboy, you saw a normal person. I can't tell you how much that means to me."

My hand went to my throat, feeling the cool silver dolphin charm. "That's why you didn't hesitate to buy this, and why you didn't want any pictures at the wedding. If you're a billionaire, then you're famous too, right?"

"I never meant to lie to you Emma. I loved the way you looked at me. I loved your honesty and how genuinely wonderful you were without knowing who I was. I'm surrounded by fake people who only want my money every moment of every day, but you, you were different. I wanted to tell you, but I was terrified you would look at me like they do."

"So you're a billionaire who spent his last vacation with a dirt-poor girl in a free hotel room," I said slowly. I moved away from him and sat down on the foot of the bed. My thoughts were racing, and every time I thought I caught one, it would slip through my fingers and speed off before I had time to process it.

"This was more than I could ever ask for," he said quietly. Jack knelt before me on the floor, his hands resting on my knees. His dark eyebrows bunched together, his face full of worry and regret.

"So what happens now?"

Jack took a deep breath. "Nothing has changed. We both knew we were going to go our separate ways. We both said we would never tell anyone about this. It's our secret, something that no one can ever take away from us. I didn't want you to pick up a magazine and find out who I was that way."

I nodded and bit my lip. I could feel tears forming and I struggled to make them stay behind my eyes. I wanted to ask him if I was merely a good time for him, or if he ached for me the way I ached for him. I was afraid it was a fling. That's all it could ever be. "I still don't want you to go, money or no money. I think I would have preferred the 'secretary is your wife' scenario. At least that way I would have known I could never have you again."

Jack smiled softly and brushed my lips with his. "I want to do something for you. If there is ever anything I can do for you, I want you to let me know. A new car perhaps?" He held a finger against my lips as I started to shake my head. "It will cost me almost nothing, but it will help you enormously. I want to see you happy Emma, and if I can help, I want to."

"I'll think about it."

"Please do. It would make me very happy to see you succeed," Jack said softly. He placed a card in my hand with a number scrawled in black ink on the back. I stuffed it into my pocket and tried to blink tears out of my eyes. I wanted to pull him into me, to make this moment not our last. I was far more attached to him than I had hoped to be.

A loud knock came at the door and Jack closed his eyes for a moment before standing. He turned silently as a second knock rapped louder. The tears escaped my eyes and trickled down my face as I stood up to follow him, grabbing his hand as he headed towards the door.

Outside a man in a black tuxedo stood waiting on the porch. Jack opened the door and nodded to him before turning back to me. His eyes were wet as his thumbs smeared the tears off my cheek. He then traced his thumb across my lower lip before taking my chin in his hand and pulling me into a kiss. I could taste the salt of my tears—salty like the ocean—as I kissed him one last time.

"This was the best vacation I'll ever have. Thank you Emma," he said softly, his eyes full of a sadness I understood too well. He started to say something more, but stopped, swallowing his words. I knew what he wanted to say because I wanted to say it out loud too—*I love you*—but it hurt too much even to think about saying it. If spoken, the pain of leaving would only be worse. This was a fling. A vacation from our lives, nothing more.

He stepped out into the bright sunshine and then my one-time husband closed the door carefully behind. I felt a piece of my heart go with him as I heard his car drive away.

CHAPTER NINE

I leaned back in my seat, wondering how my life could have changed so much and yet not changed at all. Everything felt different since I met Jack, but everything was still the same. I was going back to my normal, boring, life and in a few hours this vacation would be nothing but a memory.

A stylish blonde woman sat next to me with headphones jammed in her ears. I sighed and didn't bother trying to introduce myself again. She had plugged her ears the moment she sat down. Besides, what would I say? *Hi! How was your vacation? I had a great time on the island. I married a billionaire!* The idea made me giggle a little as she pulled out a magazine.

On the cover was a black and white photo of Jack with the tag line: Billionaire Bachelors. Seeing him took my breath away and made my insides ache. I missed him and my plane wasn't even back in the states yet. The woman flipped to the article, Jack's eyes catching me from the page. I wished I could take the magazine and hold him close to me again. I didn't expect to miss him like this. The woman gave me a dirty look for reading over her shoulder and angled the magazine away from me, flipping to a new story about a basketball star's lavish wedding.

I sighed and looked out the window. Who would ever believe that shy, cautious Emma would marry, let alone marry a billionaire on vacation? I put my own headphones on and tried to settle into the chair. It was going to be a long flight home and the ache in my heart wasn't going to speed things up. *Maybe if I fell asleep,* I thought.

I felt the plane bank slightly as I drifted off, Jack's smile filling my dreams. Time to go home.

***

The plane landed with an unceremonious *thunk*, waking me from my sleep. The captain droned on about the freezing temperatures outside and the local time, but I barely listened. The world outside the window was a frosted gray. It was snowing, providing the perfect contrast of real life to my vacation. Time to get back to reality.

I turned my phone on and sent a quick message to my friend Ashley to let her know I had landed before putting it back in my pocket and heading off the plane. My suitcase rattled behind me, as I followed a mom trying to convince her two young sons that they should put on their coats. She sounded so much like my mother that I couldn't help but smile and make sure my own hat and coat were on.

I was paying more attention to the mother's frazzled explanations about the weather than my surroundings when she fell silent as they stepped onto the moving stairs down towards baggage claim. I followed her gaze and felt my jaw drop. The normally empty greeting area at the base of the escalator was crowded with people and cameras.

"Mom, are those Pizzerias?" One of the kids asked.

"You mean 'paparazzi', and I think so. I have no idea why though. Somebody famous must be coming to town," she answered, smoothing the young boy's hair down as a flash went off.

"What if it's Goliath the Fighting Machine?" the younger son asked excitedly, turning to face his mom.

"Maybe it is. We'll check the paper when we get home. Watch your step and, Jimmy, put your coat on," the mother coaxed as the three of them stepped off the escalator. I wondered who all the fuss was about, but the photographers kept watching the stairs and taking random pictures as passengers emptied off their planes.

I was almost to the door by the baggage carousel when one of the paparazzi turned excitedly and snapped my picture. Small bright stars filled my vision from the flash, and I stumbled forward towards the door. I turned to yell at the photographer, but suddenly every photographer there seemed to be heading my way. Instinct took over and a sudden need to get out overpowered me. I wheeled to escape out the door, but two large cameras blocked my exit path.

I could see Ashley's car waiting outside the glass doors, so I lunged forward, trying to avoid the cameras suddenly appearing in front of me. Fighting through the crowd, someone pulled my hair, and I felt a pocket on my jacket rip and give way. It was hard to breathe in the mass of electronics and people, but I finally managed to escape out the automatic doors.

I threw my suitcase in the backseat of Ashley's car and jumped in the passenger seat, a wave of cameras following me out the door. Seeing the wall of people headed out the door towards her car, Ashley gunned the gas as soon as I was sitting, escaping out of the small airport.

"What the hell is going on?" I shouted, looking at my torn coat. I slammed the seat-belt in the lock and turned to Ashley. "Thanks for getting me out of there. Those people are crazy!"

Ashley grinned and tossed me a magazine. It was one of the trashy ones called *The Press* that she always picked up whenever she went grocery shopping. On the front cover was a picture of my wedding. Jack's arms were wrapped around me as he kissed me under the white awning with the headline "EXCLUSIVE!" plastered across the cover in garish red. I felt my jaw drop again. At this rate, I was going to end up with a bruise on my chest.

"They're here for you, Mrs. Saunders. I wouldn't have believed it myself if I hadn't seen the pictures. Cute dress by the way," Ashley said nonchalantly as she headed towards the highway. I looked at the picture again. It was incredibly sensual, but sweet, the way a real marriage kiss should look. "Your phone's going off by the way."

I pulled my phone out of my pocket. The ancient thing was shaking angrily as it counted up missed messages. The number rolled into over 100 missed calls with just as many voice mails, and the darn thing was still shaking as it counted. I stuffed it back into my pocket and looked at Ashley like she had something to do with it.

"I can't believe you really did it! You have to tell me all about it!" she squealed as she veered around a car going too slow for her taste. I couldn't find words and stared at the magazine. She laughed at the expression on my face and tapped her hand on the glossy cover. "Go on read it. It's today's issue. Tell me if it is all true! I can't believe you bagged Jack Saunders. Way to go Emma!" Ashley grinned at me as she turned onto the highway. The car felt suddenly hot with me bundled in my jacket and the heater on full blast, but I had a feeling it had more to do with the adrenaline and shock moving through my system. This was not what I had expected to come home to.

I opened up the magazine and flipped to the article, reading it aloud. "Playboy billionaire Jack Saunders married a homegrown girl from Iowa during his vacation to the exclusive Ocean Blue Resort on Ocean Key Island. Not much is known about this small town beauty, other than her name is Emma LaRue and she currently works as a veterinarian." I stopped and looked over at Ashley. "I don't know if you know this, but I'm not a vet."

Ashley smacked my arm with her hand and then waved it so I would continue reading. "These exclusive photos show the happy couple very much in love. Sorry ladies, this 'Prince Charming' is now off the market!"

"So, is it true?" Ashley asked excitedly as I flipped through the photos. They looked like they had been taken by someone hiding behind a bush near the wedding site. I couldn't believe how happy we both looked. The car swerved a little as she turned with an excited grin to point at the pictures.

"Eyes on the road! Well, it's sort of true. It was kind of an impulse thing. It isn't legal or anything. No one was supposed to know."

Ashley squealed with excitement and the car swerved a little again. I resisted the urge to grab the door frame and instead glared at her.

"But it really was Jack Saunders? That really is you?"

I nodded and she started jumping up and down in her seat and giggling with excitement.

"Eyes on the road, Ashley!" I yelled as the car swerved with every giggle.

"Is he as handsome in real life as he is in the pictures? Did you go out on his yacht? What parties did you go to?"

"I hate to disappoint you, but we mostly sat on the beach and talked," I said. *And he kisses like heaven and can turn my body to happy mush in 3.5 seconds.* "I actually didn't even know who he was until the last day."

"What!? You didn't recognize the most eligible billionaire bachelor? The prince that all Cinderellas are waiting for? And all you did was sit on a beach? No yacht? Are you serious?" The car swerved again.

"Road, Ashley. And no, I didn't recognize him. I don't read this stuff like you do," I said, holding up the magazine. "I knew he had money, but he seemed like a normal guy."

"Normal? Emma, honey, he is *so* much more than normal." She looked over at me like I had said that chocolate was the most disgusting food on the planet. I sighed.

"You want to tell me all about him, don't you?"

"Well, despite marrying the guy, you obviously know nothing about him." Ashley veered around an SUV and shrugged apologetically at the driver as we zoomed past.

"Okay. Tell me."

"*The Press* calls him 'The Prince'. He is the son of a super wealthy oil prospector and is set to inherit the billions that is DS Oil and Gas, as well as a bunch of other little companies his father invested in. He tries to keep a low profile, but he is considered a bit of a playboy. There is always a different model on his arm for every society function. Not a whole lot is known about him, other than his good looks, boyish charm, and that he is practically made of money. Oh, and that he loves hamburgers."

"Hamburgers, huh? I'll keep that in mind."

I stared down at the magazine in my hands. The photo was obviously taken from a distance, but it captured our kiss. I felt the ache in my chest threatening to consume me, but I couldn't look away from the photograph. I didn't see a man with wealth.

I only saw Jack. I traced my finger along the curve of his cheek, remembering the warmth of his skin.

"Rumor is his dad is sick. He wasn't supposed to take over the company until after his 31st birthday, but as you probably know, he is barely 29 and everything is going into motion to make him CEO."

"He didn't mention his dad. He said this was his last vacation before having to take over," I said quietly, my eyes glued to his photograph.

"Well, yeah. It is kind of a big deal, Emma. He has his work cut out for him. This transition wasn't supposed to take place for almost another 2 years and things are kind of a mess," Ashley said as she veered around another car. She launched into business degree mode, the passion in her life other than tabloids and reality TV. The words sounded English, but I gave up trying to understand after the word "fiscal". She had plenty to say on the subject, and I let her jabber on how difficult this particular transition was going to be while I stared at the glossy magazine pages.

"Whoa! I think somebody is at your apartment. You want to come stay at my place? Talk some more?" Ashley slowed to a stop in front of my building. Three black SUVs with tinted windows stood collecting snow in the visitor parking. I bit my lip and played with the ripped pocket on my coat. I didn't want another run in with the press like at the airport, but I didn't see much of a choice.

"I don't have anything but my suitcase full of bathing suits," I said slowly as a gust of wind flung snow at the windshield. "I'll be fine. Besides, my landlord loves calling the cops. If she gets the chance to throw somebody out, it'll make her week. Thanks for the ride though," I said, zipping my jacket up under my chin like a suit of armor.

"Okay, but if you need anything, you call. Hey, Emma,..." Ashley eyed the SUVs and then turned and gave me a hug. "Be careful okay? I know I sound all excited that you married a billionaire, but he is known as a playboy. He is responsible for a lot of broken hearts. I don't want you to get hurt."

"Aw, Ashley. Thanks. I think I'll be okay though. This was only supposed to be a vacation fling anyway. I'm sure it will all blow over in a couple of days." I gave her an extra squeeze and then pulled the collar of my jacket up to brave the cold.

"Lunch tomorrow?" Ashley asked as I prepared myself to open the door into the freezing storm.

"I have work, but what about drinks after? I'll tell you all about my trip."

Ashley beamed. "It's a date."

I fought to open the car door, the snow and ice blowing angrily around the heat of the car. I grabbed my bag and lugged it up the front steps, tucking my head like a turtle into the collar of my coat. The keys were freezing in my bare hands, but I opened the door and stepped inside, turning to wave at Ashley. No reporters yet at least.

Ashley waved back and slowly pulled out of the lot and off towards her house once she saw the front door unlock. A huge man in a black suit stood at the entrance to the hallway, but he made no move to stop me or take my picture, so I ignored him. The hall to my door seemed lonelier than usual, but my hands were too cold for me to care. I fumbled with the keys again and pushed open the door to my apartment, ready for a hot shower and some food.

CHAPTER TEN

"You made good time," an attractive woman said as I walked in the door. She stood gracefully, a fitted pinstripe suit accenting her tall frame. Her dark hair was pulled back into a tight bun, her stylish square glasses accentuating her jaw line. The door swung on its hinges behind me as I forgot to close it. The suitcase clattered to the floor and I stood there facing at the official looking woman in my living room.

"Who are you? How did you get in here? And what the hell is going on?" I wanted to scream. I wanted to run into my bedroom and lock the door. I was jet lagged and travel weary, and my head was still spinning from the airport; a stranger in my locked apartment was not something I wanted to deal with right now.

"My name is Rachel Weber. I'm Jack Saunders' personal assistant. Your landlord, Mrs. Jenkins, let me in. She was very nice, though very eager to tell me she would call the police if there was any trouble. What 'the hell' is going on is that I am here to bring you to New York." She said it as though it were all very simple and straightforward. I could feel my jaw hanging open again.

"You work for Jack?" Saying his name seemed to invoke some courage within me.

"Yes. He sent me here to come get you." Rachel smiled, looking professional and calm. I, on the other hand, felt like a nervous wreck.

"I'm afraid I don't understand," I said slowly. Rachel guided me onto the threadbare couch. It looked very drab compared to her nice suit, but I collapsed into the chair anyway.

"Due to the publicity surrounding your 'wedding', the Saunders family would like you to come out to New York until the dust has settled. Mr. Saunders sent me to personally escort you."

"But I can't go to New York. I have work tomorrow," I said. Rachel patted my knee gently.

"That has already been taken care of. Your employer was very understanding."

"But how will I make rent? I can't go. I don't have enough saved up and—" Rachel cut off my panicked sentence, her voice full of patience.

"You will be compensated for your time. Besides, you are now the wife of a billionaire. I'm afraid this is non-negotiable."

My mouth hung open for a moment as I took in what she was saying. I was going to have to leave again, *but I was going to get to see Jack!* A thrill went through me at the idea of seeing him again, followed quickly by a burst of fear. We had said our goodbyes. He had fallen for vacation me and I was now back to regular me.

"Oh. I guess I should go pack then," I said, standing. I wanted to go into my room and pretend to put things in a suitcase to give myself a moment to think. The world was spinning too quickly and I needed a minute to catch up.

"That won't be necessary. I have already packed your bags with clothing I deemed appropriate," Rachel said matter-of-factly. She inclined her head toward a small handbag by the door. It was only about the size of a plastic grocery bag. "The rest of your attire will be purchased for you in New York."

"I guess that's one way to avoid baggage fees," I murmured looking at the small bag. I sat down again, overwhelmed. This was a lot to come back to after a long flight and the way things were looking, I had more travel time in my future. "Are you the secretary that went on vacation with him?" I asked, my brain skipping like a stone on water. I could barely keep two thoughts from running into one another.

Rachel's dark brows pinched with disgust. "No. That was his *secretary*, Brandy. I'm his *personal assistant.*" She made sure to enunciate the words as though there were a very clear difference and that a personal assistant was much more important.

"Oh. Are you sure I have to go to New York?" I asked, suddenly feeling very nervous and tired. As much as I wanted to see Jack again, the idea of New York City was a bit terrifying. I really wanted to sleep for a little bit. This was all happening so fast. Rachel looked at me as though she were waiting for a child to realize that her parent's decision was final.

"Yes. Here, Mr. Saunders asked me to give this to you. He said he promised you a copy," Rachel said, handing me an envelope. I opened it carefully to find a 4x6 photograph. It was the wedding photo he had taken on his phone. I looked so happy, and he was so handsome. It was much better than all the tabloid photos. I touched his face and could almost feel his strong arms around me. For a brief moment, the joy of that moment surrounded me. I could do this. I could do this for him. I turned to Rachel and smiled, drawing strength from the photograph.

"When do we leave?"

CHAPTER ELEVEN

≈≈≈

It wasn't easy, but I convinced Rachel to let me take a quick shower, begging her to let me get warm before hopping on another plane. She finally relented and even had a PB&J sandwich ready for me when I got out. I felt better after scrubbing the travel grime out of my hair, but she had me out the door and into a dark SUV before it was even dry.

We didn't go back to the Des Moines International Airport, but instead to a small local private airport. I had driven past it a million times on my way to work, but never thought I would ever take a flight from there. We drove right up to the plane and security barely glanced at us before stepping onto the luxury jet. I sat down cautiously on an oversized leather seat that looked like it belonged in someone's living room rather than on a plane. Rachel spoke to the pilot for a moment and then sat across from me in a matching oversized chair as she powered through something on her phone.

We sat in awkward silence as the plane taxied to a runway and the engines powered up. I felt like a creature under a microscope as Rachel tapped on her phone and yet somehow watched my every move. I could tell she was evaluating me, weighing and measuring me to see if I was fit for her employer. I felt like squirming, but I held still and instead observed her.

She was tall, and not from the heels she was wearing. She had dark brown hair and infinite dark brown eyes. I guessed her age to be mid-forties, but she had an agelessness to her that made it difficult to guess. She set down her phone on the console next to her chair and pulled out a file from a bag leaning against her chair. Her face was unreadable; I decided I should never play poker with her. My lips suddenly felt very dry and I struggled not to lick them.

"I looked into you, Emma Jane LaRue of Ankeny, Iowa. Your father is a dentist, your mother his assistant and you have applied to eight veterinary schools in the past month. You won the vacation through a random call into a radio station and you have no ties to any large business." She listed off the main points of my life as though they were nothing more than a simple report. I gulped hard.

She held up the file and I could see my name stenciled neatly on a corner as she flicked through it. I wondered what the other pages could possibly contain considering how boring my life was.

"You live alone and work as a veterinary

technician at the local vet. You are not currently in a relationship and it has been some time since your last one. I know that you met Mr. Saunders on the beach during an emergency and that you handled yourself well." She paused and closed the file, setting it on her lap. "What I want to know is your intentions with my boss."

"I don't have any intentions," I answered truthfully. "I had intended to never see him again." *Except maybe in my dreams and fantasies.* "I had intended to never tell a soul what happened on my vacation. This was supposed to be a secret for the two of us— something that was supposed to be only ours that we never had to share. I have no idea how anyone got those pictures and I have no clue what I am currently doing or what I intend to do."

Rachel pursed her lips and leaned back in her chair. She settled the file back into the bag.

"Good. You are honest. I like that. He said you would be, but I wanted to see it for myself." A small smile slowly crossed her features. "I've actually never seen him smile as much as he does when he talks about you, Ms. LaRue. He gets a light in his eyes that twinkles straight from his soul."

I could see that she cared for him, like an older sister looking out for a younger brother. A little nervousness left me as I realized that she wasn't a romantic threat.

"I will be watching you Ms. LaRue, or I suppose it should be Mrs. Saunders. If you try to hurt my boss, know that I am worse than a mother lion. There will be nothing left of you. Do you understand?" The smile turned predatory. No, not a romantic threat... but still a threat.

***

Night had covered the world in darkness as we landed at another private airport. I could see the lights from the city starting to sparkle and shine, twinkling glimmers in the cold winter night. I could see a bridge I knew had to be famous lit up like a summer sky, but before I could even ask what bridge it was, Rachel was hurrying me onto a helicopter.

My interest in the bridge was quickly overpowered by the noisy machine as I climbed in and sat down. Rachel calmly put the headphones over her ears and pointed to a set for me. I couldn't help it, but my hands shook as I put them over my head. I sat glued to the window as we flew into the heart of the big city. I didn't dare blink or I would miss something. Buildings taller than my imagination emerged from the darkness as we floated through the air, the lights shone like glittering beads. The entire city looked like an elaborate piece of giant's jewelry shimmering in the dark.

After only a few moments, the helicopter landed on the roof of a building. I couldn't even guess how many stories above the ground we were, the building was far taller than anything from my hometown. Rachel carefully nudged me out of the helicopter, comfortable even with the blades whizzing above her head as she herded me toward a strong iron door. As we approached, a suited arm pushed it open and we stepped inside.

The quiet of the stairs hummed after the noise of the helicopter engine. I could feel my hands still shaking, but I tried my best to hide it from Rachel. I never thought I would ride on a helicopter, but I certainly thought I could get used to it.

The suited man who had opened the door escorted us to a large wooden desk with the DS Oil and Gas logo printed on the wall behind it. It was well after the end of a normal workday, so no secretary sat in the chair, but Rachel walked past it to a large doorway with two giant wooden panels. She knocked confidently once, and motioned me over. I stumbled over my feet, but made it next to her by the time a voice called out to come in.

Rachel turned and straightened my jacket, brushing several flyaway strands of hair out of my face before giving me a quick smile and opening the door. She stepped in confidently, and I followed, trying desperately to mimic her confidence. I suddenly realized I had no idea what I was going to say to him.

Jack sat at a large mahogany desk, papers and electronic pads scattered haphazardly across the large wooden surface. His back was to the door, a phone up to his ear as he spoke in a clipped voice. Every word oozed dominance and surety. This wasn't the boy I met on the beach. That voice didn't laugh and giggle, drinking margaritas in the sand. The man in front of me was cold and full of authority and power.

The phone conversation ended, and he turned abruptly to face the two of us, annoyance and fatigue painted on his face. However, as soon as he saw who had invaded his office, that smile I knew lit up his features. I could see the Jack I met on the beach in that smile, the business man banished to the shadows for a moment.

"I expect you two had an uneventful trip? Good," he said as he stood and began to walk around the desk. "Thank you Rachel. I'm sure you have things that need to be taken care of."

"Yes, Sir," Rachel said formally. She turned, and as she passed me on the way to the door she said quietly, "I'll be at the desk down the hall to the right when you are finished."

I nodded shallowly, unsure of what was going to happen next, and I bit my lip as I watched her close the door carefully behind her before turning to face Jack.

"I'm sorry to have caused you so much trouble," I said quickly. He stopped in his tracks, shaking his head and smiling.

"If anything, I should be the one apologizing to you. If I were a normal person, this never would have been front page news."

"I'm still sorry that this must be a press nightmare for you. How did they get those pictures?" I asked quietly. He finished walking around to the front of his massive desk and leaned against it, crossing his arms and looking at me with dark eyes.

"My secretary. The one who came on the trip. She was angry and looking for a way to make me pay." His eyes somehow darkened further, turning into deep pools with no bottom. "She is no longer in my employ."

"What are we going to do?" I asked. There was a space between us. It wasn't more than a couple of feet, but it felt like miles. We were two very different people. He was wearing designer pants and a button up shirt, the suit jacket carelessly hanging on the back of his chair. The jacket alone was probably worth more than my car. I stood in sale-priced shoes and a torn coat, wondering what in the world was going to happen next.

Jack sighed and his arms tightened. I wanted to touch those muscles again, but at the same time, he was so different from the man on the beach, I wasn't sure if I could. He spoke easily, as though I were a client and this wasn't our lives, but instead a business transaction.

"My father is furious. He feels that this celebrity status is distracting from business and distracting me from my work. He holds no animosity towards you, but this is not how he planned this transition to go. He wants to do nothing, to let it all blow over and focus on the transition," Jack stopped and caught my eye. "But I couldn't leave you to the mercy of the paparazzi hounds by yourself though. You will be staying with me in my home and under the safety of my security team. I heard the paparazzi were a bit rough with you at the airport."

I realized I was playing with the torn pocket of my jacket and I quickly dropped it. "I'll live. Thank you though."

"This should all blow over soon. I want to make sure you are safe. I don't want anything to happen to you, Emma."

My name on his lips made my body go warm. Something uncoiled deep in the pit of my stomach, asking for more, but before I could decide what to do, the phone began to ring. Jack glared at it for a second before leaning over and answering it curtly. He listened for a moment and then told the caller to wait a moment as he pushed a button and set it on the desk.

He was across the room to where I stood in less than two strides. "I have to get back to work, but I want you to know that I'm glad you're here Emma. Despite the circumstances, I'm glad." I could hear the truth in his voice and I couldn't help but smile. I was glad to be here too.

Jack leaned forward, pressing his lips against mine. This kiss wasn't the same as the ones from the island. This was reserved and formal, but it still fanned the heat growing inside of me. He stepped back, a devilish grin spreading across his face as I flushed. The smile stayed on his face until he sat down in the large leather chair and picked up the phone. I knew that was my cue to leave, and I slipped out the door as the businessman's mask slid over his face.

CHAPTER TWELVE

Jack's home was the most beautiful living space I had ever seen. It was as if a giant had placed a fully furnished house on top of a skyscraper. The entryway was dark, but I could see city lights through the towering glass windows in the main room. Rachel closed the door softly behind me and offered to take my jacket. I shrugged out of it, glad the room was warm after the cold March air outside. I stood, glancing around, trying to figure out how big Jack's home really was.

"There are three bedrooms, an office, a dining room, living room, and the kitchen. There is a pool on the terrace, but it is currently empty due to the weather. The hot tub is open though," Rachel said, reading my mind. I gulped slightly. This was bigger than my parents' house and it was sixteen stories in the air. "I'll show you your room."

Rachel guided me into the main living room across hardwood floors. The furniture was sleek and modern, but it felt comfortable. As we walked into the room, a gentle light turned on making it easy to navigate but not bright enough to cause glare on the floor-to-ceiling windows.

"That's the Statue of Liberty," I whispered, drawn to the windows like a child. I wanted to press my hands up against the glass and peer outside, but I only managed to gape and stare out the window. I never thought in a million years I would ever walk into a place with views like this.

"Yes. If you'd like, I can arrange a sightseeing tour of the city for you." Rachel stood watching me, a bemused smile on her face.

"That would be amazing! I don't know how much it would cost, but I would love to see Central Park and Times Square too," I said, pulling myself away from the window. Rachel laughed.

"Cost is no issue. Jack has made it very clear that you are to have anything you want, no matter the price. You are, technically speaking, the wife of a billionaire."

My tongue felt very dry. The most I had ever had in my bank account at one time was a little over five thousand dollars, and that had only lasted until I paid tuition. The idea that I didn't need to worry about money was slightly intimidating. Rachel tipped her head, motioning me to follow.

"I realize that this must all be very new for you, Emma. I'll help you as much as I can. If you need anything or want anything, please let me know. Mr.

Saunders has put me at your disposal for as long as you are in New York." She turned and smiled, pushing open a door to reveal a large bedroom. "This is your room."

I stepped inside. The room was probably as big as my entire apartment back home. A beautiful king-sized bed sat in the middle of the room on an island of plush carpet surrounded by hardwood floors. Another floor to ceiling window dominated the far wall, a sheer curtain currently obscuring the view. A writing desk was tucked in the corner next to a wooden dresser, and I could see a bathroom bigger than my parents' kitchen through an attached doorway.

"Your clothes are in the closet, and everything you need is in the bathroom. If you're hungry, the kitchen is fully stocked. Mr. Saunders will be staying at the office tonight, so you have the place to yourself. Will breakfast at eight be acceptable?" Rachel stepped back into the doorway, clasping her hands behind her back. I realized that it was late and she was probably ready for bed.

"That should be fine. Um, if I need something in the middle of the night, who should I call? Is there a number for the landlord I should know?"

Rachel's lip twitched up in amusement. "No, no landlord. If you need anything, you have my phone number. My apartment is just downstairs, so I'm not far away. There is also a security guard outside at all times that can assist you with anything you may need in the night."

"Then I will see you at eight tomorrow," I said. A

yawn snuck out at the very end, my body suddenly realizing that I was tired. Rachel nodded briskly and headed down the hallway. I heard her close the door behind her.

Suddenly, I was very tired... and very alone. I quickly got ready for bed and cuddled into the downy-softness of the big bed. Sleep found me quickly and fell into it deep.

***

I woke to a gray dawn leaking in through the gauzy curtain. Outside, I could see the Hudson River flowing past a cold world. Gray buildings reached up towards a gray sky, the city skyline stretching as far as I could see. The city was so much bigger than anything I had ever seen and I felt tiny in comparison. I was very far from home.

I slipped on some clothes and headed to the kitchen. Rachel would be arriving any minute, but I was starving so I poured a glass of milk and sat at the comfortable wooden kitchen table, looking out at the city skyline and wondering what crazy thing was going to happen today.

My thoughts were interrupted by a sharp knock on the door, followed by Rachel calling my name. She found me in the kitchen and handed me a foil wrapped burrito.

"I had Maria make yours mild, but if you like spicier, she makes a mean salsa," Rachel said as she sat down across from me and unwrapped a matching burrito. She set a container of salsa in the center of the table. I carefully pulled the foil off my own burrito and took a bite.

"This is fantastic," I moaned as I stuffed my face full of eggs, potatoes, cheese and tortilla. Rachel grinned and nodded as she took a bite out of her own.

"Maria, the head maid, makes these from scratch. I have yet to find a restaurant that makes them this good. Try it with the salsa."

I poured a little on the top and took a bite. My mouth flooded with spicy deliciousness. It was the perfect level of heat so I poured more on. Before I knew it, I was licking the last bits off my fingers. "So what are we doing today?" I asked, wishing I had more burrito. I was full, but it had been so tasty.

"We are going to dress you like a billionaire's wife. I hope you are ready for a busy day," Rachel answered, folding up the foil to her own burrito. I tried not to sigh too loudly. I hated shopping. Nothing ever seemed to fit properly and I always ended up spending too much for things I only sort of liked.

We stood up from the table and headed to the door. Rachel frowned at my ripped coat as I threw it on over my long-sleeved t-shirt. "What?" I asked.

"We have our work cut out for us today," she said with a forced smile.

I shrugged and opened the door, nearly running into a tall, dark-haired man. I sputtered an apology and stepped back into the apartment, hoping he was supposed to be there and wasn't a very clever tabloid reporter.

"Hello, Dean. Is the car ready?" Rachel asked him smoothly as she buttoned her coat and stepped around him into the hallway. He nodded. "Excellent. Dean, I would like to introduce you to Ms. Emma LaRue. Emma, this is Dean Sherman. He will be your personal security consultant while you are here in New York."

"Personal security consultant? You mean I get a bodyguard?"

Dean grinned at me. He was tall and thin, but I could tell he was far stronger than he looked. His dark hair held traces of gray, but his blue eyes were bright and piercing. He held out his hand and when I shook it, there was genuine warmth in his grasp.

"Ms. LaRue, it is a pleasure to meet you. Your safety is my priority, so I will be following you at all times. I do my best to be discreet, but if there is a situation, I will need you to follow my directions." I nodded and he let go of my hand.

"Are you sure I need a bodyguard? I mean, no offense, but I'm not that important."

Dean gave me a look that could match my father's. "You *are* important, and Mr. Saunders agrees with me. So no trying to lose me because you don't think you need a bodyguard." If he was anything like my father, he was about to start explaining to me something he felt was important.

"I would never—" I started.

"We'll go over your rules in the car, Dean," Emma cut in, hustling me down the hallway. "We're on a tight schedule today."

"Of course Ms. Weber," Dean said smoothly,

tipping his head. "As you wish."

Rachel gave him a brief smile before shooing me into the elevator. A shiny black SUV was waiting in the garage. Dean slid gracefully into the front seat as Rachel and I took the back seat. Once inside, Rachel and Dean went through a list of rules to keep me safe. It was mostly common sense and making sure that Dean could always see me. He made sure I had his phone number and gave me several ways to get his attention if I felt I needed him to be closer. I liked Dean. The way he spoke reminded me of my father and it was comforting to know he was looking out for me.

The car pulled up in front of a chic looking tall building with red awnings. Rachel grinned at me as we exited the vehicle and stepped into the luxurious store. Shoes that made my mouth water and feet ache just by looking at the heels, purses with names that I only associated with movie stars, and gleaming racks of beautiful clothes stood in front of me. I picked up a small bag, thinking it was kind of pretty and glanced at the price tag. $5,950. I set it down slowly, afraid it might break if I touched it too roughly.

"Rachel! They said you were coming today. How wonderful to see you! Is there anything in particular you are looking for?" A friendly voice drew my attention away from the designer clutch purse. A fashionably dressed woman was smiling at Rachel. She looked at me for a moment as though she recognized me, but couldn't place from where.

"Hello, Kristine. I need to purchase some basics for Ms. LaRue. "Rachel smiled politely at her, and the woman's eyes flashed with recognition.

"LaRue? Jack's beach bride Emma LaRue..." The woman's voice trailed off as she realized she was quoting a tabloid magazine. She suddenly looked at me in a very different manner. "Of course. Let me get the room set up for you!"

Rachel turned and faced me. She ran her eyes up and down, eying me like a blank canvas she was preparing to paint. I tried not to fidget.

"Hmm, I think the spring collection will suit you wonderfully. Come with me," Rachel said with a grin. I could tell she was in her element, as she headed into a rack of clothes and started pulling out different designs and patterns. She would hold one up, evaluate, and then either put it back or drape it over the waiting arm of Kristine.

"Do you prefer comfort or color?" She asked briskly.

"Comfort. Definitely comfort."

"Are you comfortable in a dress? What lengths?"

"I guess so. I don't wear them very often, but they're fine. I like the knee length ones. Too short and my legs get sticky when I sit on things."

Rachel nodded, asking questions as she moved through the racks adding more clothes to the growing pile in the saleswoman's arms. "I think we have a good starting point," she said finally.

I reluctantly followed the other two women to the dressing area. We were in our own separate room, filled with mirrors and a comfortable looking chair outside the changing area, a space obviously reserved for exclusive customers. Rachel selected an assortment of dresses, slacks and blouses, handing them to me with no order I could see. I walked into the changing area, glancing over my shoulder as she settled into the chair.

I looked at the clothes with dread. I hated trying on clothes. Hated it! It was something I did only in the most dire situations and even then as quickly as possible. I could hear Kristine offer Rachel something to drink, and Rachel requesting some sandwiches as well. We were going to be here for a while. There was no way I was going to get out of trying them on, and besides, I had no clothes back at the penthouse.

With a sigh of resignation, I pulled off my clothes, neatly folding them on the small bench and tried on the first dress. To my surprise, it fit better than I expected. It was a simple wool dress, but it actually seemed to fit.

"The purple one fits," I called out.

"Let me see," Rachel replied. I sighed. I could tell she was going to have to look at everything I tried on. This was going to be a painful few hours. I took a deep breath and opened the door.

"The color is definitely good, but we need a different cut. Kristine, will you get the one with the square cut?" Rachel frowned thoughtfully and then smiled. "These are going to look so amazing on you. Go ahead and forget the rest of the dresses and skip to the slacks. Try the black ones first. I think you'll like the cut."

I returned to the changing room, and slipped out of the dress glancing at the fluttering price tag. $1,895! For a dress? The number made my head spin and I hung the dress up very carefully. I knew that kind of money would be nothing to the Saunders' bank account, but it was still way more than I had in mine.

I slid the pants on and wanted to shout for joy. They fit. Actually fit. And they made my butt look good. And my front. Holy cow did I like these pants! This never happened while shopping by myself. Pants that fit on the first try? I didn't hesitate this time, opening the door to show Rachel.

"Nice! How do they feel?" Rachel asked, standing up and walking over. I turned slowly so she could see the pants.

"They feel amazing."

"I thought these would be perfect for you. Oh, you are going to be fun to shop for! You are going to be able to pull off some amazing styles." Rachel was grinning from ear to ear.

"What do you mean? I usually can't find anything that looks good," I said slowly.

"That's because you didn't have me," she replied. There was a light in her eyes, a simple happiness in helping me find clothes that was contagious.

"I'm guessing you like to shop," I said.

Rachel nodded as she walked around me, rechecking the pants. Rachel laughed. "I like shopping. I love fashion. In fact, 'love' might not be strong enough to describe how much I enjoy fashion." She motioned me back towards the dressing room, handing me a blue dress from her collection. "Try on this one—I want to see it on you."

I stepped back into the dressing room and slid out of the pants and shirt and into a blue satin sheath dress. It felt like luxury. "Why do you like fashion? I guess I've never seen the appeal."

"I like the art of it. At its core, it's a way to make the world more beautiful. Now, I don't go for the stick-thin model and I don't have this or that designer because he's 'the designer' of the month. For me, it's an art form. The way clothes can bring out a person's personality and moods. I love finding beauty in the fabrics and styles that fit a person. It's like painting a walking canvas with a million different kinds of brushes and paints. I can dress you for an occasion, a mood, an emotion, anything, but the fun is finding things that work for the individual and creating something beautiful out of the pieces. It must be tailored to the individual or it won't work. Something that works for one person, will never work for another." Her enthusiasm was evident in her voice. It made me smile.

"You make it sound glamorous and interesting. I hate to say it, but I've never thought of clothes like that."

"Most people don't. Certain aspects of it have been so commercialized that it has become more about the money than the design." She looked sheepish for a moment. "I'll admit that having access to a billionaire's pocketbook does make it easier to afford some of the more unique pieces, but today, part of getting these clothes for you is getting the brand recognition. We want people to associate you with the wealth of that designer. So, in this instance, the money is actually part of the design."

"Sounds like I'm being encouraged to get the

expensive thing then, I guess. That's a first for me!" I laughed and smoothed the fabric across my hips. It hung nicely across my hips, but was baggy where it was obviously meant to fit someone with a much bigger bust.

"You obviously know a lot about all this. How did you end up a personal assistant? Is fashion a prerequisite course at personal assistant school?" I asked as I opened the door and stepped out. Rachel looked me up and down, murmuring to herself before answering my question.

"I like it, but it will need some tailoring," Rachel said absentmindedly as she pulled the fabric tight in the back and I could practically hear her smile as she thought about how it would look. She nodded to herself and then raised her eyes to mine. "I majored in fashion and design in college. One of my senior designs caught the eye of Mrs. Saunders. To make a long story short, I ended up entwining myself with the Saunders family. When Jack needed a personal assistant, he hired me. Now try this one," she said handing me a bright red shirt.

I took the brightly colored shirt and headed back to the dressing room. "So, do you still design clothes then?"

"Sometimes. I've made a couple of exclusive garments for the Saunders family, but Mr. Saunders keeps me too busy to devote much time to it," she answered. A hint of sadness crept into her voice at the end. I wondered how much she missed it and if she felt it was worth it. She continued, as if reading my mind. "I miss it, but I like my job. This though, this is fun. Mr. Saunders lets me control his wardrobe, but the female stuff is so much more fun."

I stepped out of the dressing room again. I hadn't had this much fun trying on clothes since I was a kid in my mom's closet. I felt pretty in these clothes, and I knew Rachel was enjoying dressing me. I opened the door and Rachel made a face.

"Not that one. The color and cut aren't going to work."

"I didn't think it looked too bad," I said confused. I had liked the shirt in the mirror.

"It doesn't look bad Emma, but it doesn't look *amazing*. I want you to look amazing. See how it bunches in the shoulders? And it brings out too much red in your face. If it were a little darker and cut differently it would work, but not like this," she said as she pointed out the bunching on my shoulders. I hadn't even noticed until she showed me. She handed me another shirt and waited for me to change. "See? This one works."

I looked in the mirror as she pointed out how the shoulders now lay flat, and the slight difference in red against my skin. The new shirt really did look better.

"Thank you," I said, meeting her eyes in the mirror. She grinned.

"You are most welcome. How do you feel about sweaters?"

"They should be warm." I grinned at her in the mirror. She laughed.

"I think we'll get along fine. I have some ideas I want to try," Rachel said, her eyes going distant as she thought of the possibilities of how she could dress me.

CHAPTER THIRTEEN

Rachel had me try on what felt like every piece of clothing in the store. I didn't mind though. With her artistic eye, it was actually fun to try things on. She made sure to pick things that were always in my size, or at least close enough that I didn't get the frustration I usually did trying on clothes. She picked out things I would never have thought to wear on my own, but I was constantly amazed at how good they looked in the mirror.

I tried not to look at the price tags. A single shirt cost a month's salary and some of the dresses made me feel woozy thinking about how many times I could pay rent with a single garment.

Rachel made sure I had everything I could possibly need. We spent the next three days perfecting my look, getting measured for custom clothing, and picking up more clothes than would fit in my closet at home. I even got real French lingerie.

The only thing I insisted on was keeping my current pajamas. Rachel tried her best to convince me that a new pair of embroidered satin pajamas would be far preferable to my very comfy scrub pants and t-shirt.

"But I like my current pajamas! I don't want new ones. Besides, anyone who sees me in my pajamas shouldn't be worrying about whether or not I look like I belong with a billionaire," I told her.

"What about Mr. Saunders?" She asked, raising her eyebrows and clearly expecting me to relent.

"Who says I will be wearing pajamas with Mr. Saunders?"

She let me keep my scrub pants and t-shirt.

I stepped out into the cold, March, New York air and took a deep breath. It smelled different here, the scents of cars, food, and cement all different than the city smells from Des Moines. I still couldn't get over how big the city was and I had a feeling I never would. I pulled up the collar of my new jacket against the wind and headed towards the waiting car.

Dean smiled and opened the door for me as I stepped into the warm car. He ran around to the passenger seat and slid inside, moving stealthily like a hunting cat. As soon as his door shut, the driver pulled out onto the busy street and merged with a sea of yellow cabs.

"Off to visit Mr. Saunders today?" Dean asked, turning in his seat to look at me. I could feel the blush creeping onto my cheeks as I nodded.

"I haven't seen him since I arrived. Rachel says he

has been working nonstop at the office, so I thought I would surprise him."

Dean's face clouded for a moment. His mouth made a twist, like he was going to tell me bad news. "So, his secretary doesn't know you are coming? This may not be the best idea Emma."

Indignation flared up in my stomach. *His secretary?* His secretary was the reason I was in this mess in the first place. I was away from my home, my friends, and my family because a secretary released a picture. I was here because Jack wanted me here and no secretary was going to stop me. I bit down a flippant remark and smiled instead.

"I want to see Jack. He's the reason I'm here and it feels weird sleeping at his house and eating his food, but never seeing him."

Dean frowned, but nodded and turned back in his seat. He wore the 'she's got to make her own mistakes' expression that my dad wore whenever I was about to do something stupid. I sighed, suddenly feeling a little less confident. I was going to see Jack today, even if it meant breaking the rules.

The rest of the drive was uneventful, the city flying past in shades of gray and glass. The DS Oil and Gas building quickly loomed up in front of us, a tower lost in a sea of murky sky. Dean opened the door and I stepped out, the air colder than I remembered. I hurried though the big glass doors and into the yellow warmth of the lobby.

Business suits swam around me like a school of giant black and gray fish as I worked my way towards a security desk. I stepped up to the desk and a man in an imposing uniform glared down at me. I was about to speak when Dean stepped up. The security guard broke out in a smile, completely changing his features from scary to pleasant.

"Dean! How's it going?" The big guard greeted Dean. Dean leaned up against the counter, his frame shielding me from the people entering and exiting the elevators.

"Doing good. I want to introduce you to Emma LaRue. She is to have full access to Jack Saunders' floor."

The big man smiled at me, suddenly friendly. "Nice to meet you Ms. LaRue. Or will it be Mrs. Saunders?"

"Emma is fine," I said. I wasn't sure myself.

"Of course Ms. Emma. Let me get you a badge. I believe Ms. Weber had one made for you already." The man ducked under the desk and unlocked a cabinet. He reappeared with an official looking badge with my picture smiling on the front. "This should get you onto his floor. The rest is up to you and his new secretary. Dean, you'll show her the way it works, won't you?"

"Of course. Thanks Jim," Dean said. The big guard waved and replaced his friendly smile with the threatening frown as Dean guided me towards green elevators. I stayed close to him, not wanting to lose my guide. We stepped onto a green elevator with several other people and Dean hit the highest button, 27. I was sure that Jack's office was higher than that, but I didn't say anything.

We stepped out at our stop and Dean led me

around a corner to another elevator. This one was golden instead of green.

"If you come in through the front door, this is the path you should take. The main elevators don't go up to the higher floors for security reasons." He hit the button for the gold doors and we stepped inside. "Scan your card against the button there and then press the 45 button. If you don't scan your card, the elevator won't move and security will be called."

I held the card up to the reader and a green light blinked. I hit 45 and the elevator whizzed upward. It took only a couple of seconds for the doors to open into the lobby I recognized from my first night. It was more brightly lit than in the evening, and there was a hum of energy. A man and a woman in expensive suits hurried past toward the offices, deep in discussion. An older woman sat at the big desk, speaking confidently into her headset.

Dean caught my arm. "This elevator goes down to the garage. If you come in through the garage, you can take this without having to get off as you would if you use the main elevators. I will be over there when you're ready to leave." He pointed to some comfortable looking leather chairs in the lobby by the secretary's desk. I swallowed hard, my mouth dry. Now that I was actually up here, my courage had disappeared.

I took a steadying breath and headed towards the big desk guarding Jack's office. The woman looked up at me as I approached and smiled kindly.

"You must be Emma. I'm Jeanette. It's a pleasure to finally meet you," she greeted me warmly. I smiled at her. She was probably in her early sixties, but despite the gray of her hair, she showed no signs of slowing down.

"Hi, it's nice to meet you too. I would like to see Jack please," I said politely.

"I'm afraid he's in a meeting right now. I would be happy to let him know you stopped by though."

"I can wait. I'd really like to see him." I didn't come all the way to his office to be stopped at the threshold by a secretary. Besides, how long could a meeting take?

Jeanette sighed. "The meeting is scheduled for another three hours. He's meeting with investors. If you would like, I can schedule you in to see him tomorrow."

"What if I just peeked my head in the door?" Frustration was starting to build. I gave serious thought to barging past the secretary and opening his office door, but knew I was too chicken to actually do it.

"I'm afraid he's not in the building for this meeting. He is meeting them downtown. I'm very sorry Ms. LaRue. If I had known you were coming, I would have scheduled something." Jeanette looked apologetic, but I felt ridiculous. I should have known better. Jack was a busy man, he wouldn't be sitting in his office waiting for me to show up.

"Thank you for your time, Jeanette. Will you let him know I stopped by?" Jeanette nodded and smiled understandingly at me. "I guess I'll go say hi to Rachel."

"Ms. LaRue, I'm afraid Rachel isn't here either.

She went with Mr. Saunders to the meeting."

"Oh, I see. Thank you for telling me." I stood there for a moment, unsure of what to do next. I thanked Jeanette again and headed slowly back towards the golden elevators.

"I'm sorry that didn't work out like you expected, Emma," Dean said softly behind me as the golden doors opened. Dean hit the button marked garage.

"Did you know? Did you know they wouldn't be here?"

"No. I don't know their schedules. I suspected they wouldn't be available, but I didn't know." Dean sounded earnest, but I still felt like he had let me fail on purpose. Resentment was bubbling up inside of me. I was in New York, away from the people and things I knew, because Jack wanted me here, but he was too busy to see me. Rachel was too busy to see me. Everyone I knew in this new place was too busy with their lives to care that I didn't have one.

The doors opened to the waiting car with tinted windows. Dean opened the door for me again.

"Where to, Miss?" asked the driver.

I didn't have an answer. I didn't want to go back to Jack's empty apartment. I didn't want to sit up there watching TV and eating food by myself. I had eaten dinner by myself every night after Rachel and I had finished shopping and I was tired of it.

"The Statue of Liberty," I blurted out. I could see it out the window from Jack's apartment and it was something to see. If I was going to have to entertain myself, I was at least going to get some sightseeing done.

"I don't know if that's such a good idea," Dean countered before the driver moved the car.

"Why not? What do you suggest then?" I tried my best not to sound defensive, but I was pretty sure I failed.

"It's a crowded place and I don't have the manpower to properly protect you. These things need to be planned, Emma," Dean said. He sounded like my father and it made me angry.

"Then tell me what I can do! I can't see Jack. I can't go sightseeing. I'm tired of shopping and I don't want to go back to an empty apartment. I'm not going to sit in Jack's house like a pretty bird in a cage. If that's all I'm going to do, I might as well go home where I at least know some people!" I wanted to scream. My world felt off kilter. I wanted to go home and have my life be familiar again.

Dean waited a moment before answering. "I know you want to do something. How about the Met? I can give you a tour. I'm familiar with the building and the security there will make me feel more comfortable."

"You mean the art museum? You know enough about the art museum to give me a tour?"

"I know enough to give the curator a tour. It'll be fun," he coaxed.

"Won't it be super crowded? Just like the Statue of Liberty?"

"It's a weekday, and at this hour it won't be busy. I can promise the tour will be amazing." He raised his eyebrows up, his face bright as he tried to convince me, "There's a sphinx and a mummy."

"Fine. We'll go look at art. It's better than sitting in

the apartment," I said with a pout. I had never been big on museums and knew next to nothing about art, but from the information I had gleaned from the TV, I knew it was a place I should see.

"To the Met!" Dean shouted, pointing his arm like he was charging into battle. I felt a smile crack my frown, but I still wasn't happy.

The car glided forward into the city traffic, and I leaned my head against the cold glass. Dean started talking about all the exhibits at the museum, his passion for the place obvious. It wasn't my first choice of activity, but I was willing to give it a chance. I half listened to him talk about the museum as I looked out the window at the giant buildings whizzing past.

Looking out at the cold gray city, I felt a sadness growing in my chest. I didn't want to be here anymore. I was homesick. I wanted my mom's cooking, a coffee from the shop on my way to work, to walk the dogs staying overnight at the vet's office. I wanted to be able to go wherever I wanted and not have a bodyguard telling where I could go and what I could do... , but I was here and I couldn't leave.

I pressed my forehead into the glass, trying to merge into it. If I were glass, I wouldn't care. I wouldn't be in this strange situation, surrounded by people I didn't know. If I were glass, I wouldn't care that the only people I knew in the city other than my bodyguard, were too busy to see me. If I were glass, then these safety measures would make sense.

"We're almost there," Dean said, breaking into my thoughts. I roused myself from the window, and actually looked out at the buildings. A giant stone building, more beautiful than any building I had ever seen, caught my attention. It looked like a place where beautiful things should be kept.

The car slowed and Dean jumped out first, helping me onto the sidewalk. I barely noticed the car move away as I gravitated towards the wide steps leading towards the entrance.

I was about halfway up the steps when the clouds broke open and a stream of sunshine cascaded onto the stairs. I closed my eyes and basked in the warmth for a moment, letting the beauty of the building and the glimmer of sunshine raise my spirits. For a moment, I thought this day could be salvaged. This could be a good day.

"Hey, it's the billionaire chick—Emma LaRue! Take her picture!" Someone shouted, throwing me out of my moment. I heard a camera click and I opened my eyes, glancing around for Dean. I wasn't worried about one person taking my picture, but my moment of peace had been shattered. I turned to head into the museum and the sun ducked back behind the clouds, the world plunging back into shades of gray.

Another flash went off, and two more. Dean was hurrying down the stairs, his face dark. He looked like an angry mother bear, ready to rip the heads off the people messing with his cub. The wind was suddenly cold and I felt a tremor of apprehension. I turned to see several taxis releasing people with cameras, and all heading straight for me.

Dean was at my side, pulling me down the stairs

towards the street. The cameras were all around me, their lenses in my face. I couldn't move forward, the cameras all flashing and circling like sharks. They were calling my name, yelling questions and trying to get my attention. I clung to Dean, lost in a sea of cameras and shouting.

"How's he fuck?" yelled one photographer, his camera close enough to make me shy away to avoid hitting it with my face. I felt my cheeks go hot. I turned to get away, but I was surrounded by cameras. I felt like I was in a lightning storm, the flashes making it hard to see. I tripped on one of the stone steps, and I would have crashed into the ground if Dean hadn't reached out and caught my arm.

He pushed his way down the stairs, towing me behind in his wake. I was so overwhelmed I followed him blindly, unsure of what was going on. Nothing could have prepared me for the onslaught of flashes and questions.

The black SUV peeled up to the corner, and Dean practically tossed me inside, slamming the door behind me. The camera flashes glared off the window and I fell forward as the car accelerated away.

"Put your seat-belt on," Dean growled as the driver darted around a taxi. "You okay?"

"What just happened?" My voice cracked. Adrenaline was pumping through my system and I couldn't figure out if I wanted to run or cry.

"Someone tipped them off. They've been hungry for pictures of you since they found out you were in New York," Dean said. His voice had lost the smiling quality. "They're still following us."

I looked back and could see several cabs jockeying for position behind us. I buckled my seat-belt, feeling the car accelerate underneath me, weaving in and out of the traffic. I was glad I wasn't the one driving.

"But why now? I've been out in the city with Rachel every day and they haven't done this." I gripped the car door as we took a tight turn.

"Those were organized trips. We cleared them with the stores ahead of time. Didn't you notice no one else was shopping?"

"I thought that was because the prices were so high. I didn't realize it was for me." I slouched in my seat. I felt like an idiot for not noticing earlier that every trip with Rachel had been carefully timed and organized.

Dean looked back at me, his eyes darting to look through the back window. "Rachel didn't want to say anything because it was pretty obvious you already felt out of place here. But you should know now. The tabloids are clamoring for pictures. You are the hot topic right now and they want you. They're offering some high prices for pictures and that means they are watching every move you make."

"What do I do?" I asked. I felt helpless. This was way out of my comfort level.

"You don't have to do anything. Just let me do my job," Dean said. He smiled kindly at me. "Don't you worry. We've lost them."

"I guess that means my trip to the Met is off for the day. No mummies for me."

"Unfortunately." He sounded more disappointed than I did. "I can take you tomorrow though if you like. I'll even get Ms. Weber to come have lunch with us."

"You promise the best tour ever?"

Dean laughed, his demeanor back to the watchful yet relaxed status I was used to. "The best tour that museum has ever seen."

"You have yourself a deal then," I said with a nod. Dean turned back around and I leaned back in my seat.

I understood now why we had to schedule things. I didn't like it, but I understood. Something about a schedule tickled at my brain. Perhaps I could get onto Jack's schedule. An idea began to form. I pulled out my phone and opened a text message to Rachel.

CHAPTER FOURTEEN

I checked my reflection in the golden doors of the elevator, feeling nervous. The food cart behind me filled the elevator with delicious smells and my stomach grumbled. I had been too nervous to eat earlier, and now I was starving.

The doors opened with a ding and I pulled the cart with two dinners behind me into the big lobby on Jack's floor. Jeannette looked up and smiled as I approached her giant desk.

"You look lovely Emma. Jack has been looking forward to dinner all day, but don't tell him I told you. He should be finishing up signing some papers, so you can go on in." She gave me a wink as I headed towards the big office doors and said, "I'll be leaving in a little bit so don't you two worry about me out here."

My mouth suddenly filled with dust and I licked my lips nervously as I reached the big doors. I hadn't seen Jack since arriving in New York. It was still a dreamlike idea that I could be here, that any of this could be happening. My brain was still having a hard time believing that he would still be interested in me, even though our vacation was over. My world had been turned upside down and I was still struggling to catch up. After my run-in with the paparazzi the day before, I wasn't sure what to expect anymore.

With a deep breath, I knocked and pushed open the heavy doors. They swung inward easily, and I pulled the cart of food quietly behind me. Jack looked up from his desk, the mask of a businessman slipping away as soon as he saw me. The boyish glint I remembered from the beach shone in his eyes. He signed the last piece of paper on his desk in a hurry and stacked it neatly on the corner before coming around to greet me.

There was an awkward moment where neither one of us was sure what we were supposed to do. Did we hug? Did we kiss? Shake hands? I went for a hug and he kissed me softly on the cheek. My heart pounded in my chest, threatening to shake my entire body.

"Jeannette said you came by yesterday," he said, breaking away from me. I wanted him to keep touching me, but I wasn't sure my nerves could handle it. I felt like a girl meeting her crush behind the school for the first time.

"Yeah, I didn't know you weren't going to be here. I'm learning the importance of scheduling," I replied. I played with the food tray, wheeling it back and forth.

"I'm sorry I missed you. I just realized that I haven't seen you since you got here and that was a couple of days ago," Jack said, leaning back against his desk.

"You've been busy, I get it. You're important."

"That isn't a very good excuse," he said, shaking his head. His hair gleamed in the soft light from his desk, and it took all my will power not to run my fingers through it. He shrugged and gestured to the food. "You hungry?"

"Starving actually," I answered. He came beside me and pushed the cart towards a couch and coffee table in the corner of his office. As he took the cart, he brushed against me, sending shivers down my spine. My body ached to remember how he felt, the way he moved inside of me. The beginnings of a blush tried to sneak onto my face, but I tried to mimic Jack's easy nonchalance and it seemed to keep the heat down lower.

He carefully placed each of the plates on the small table, motioning me to sit down. I sat gingerly on the leather sofa, my stomach doing flip flops. I couldn't understand my anxiety; I had slept with the man, but now, now that we were going to actually have to get to know one another, I was nervous. Jack had met vacation me. Vacation me was bold and did crazy things like marrying strangers.

Unfortunately, vacation me lived in the Caribbean, not New York. Now I was New York me and I suspected New York me was pretty much the same as Iowa me. The cautious boring me that didn't know how to have a boyfriend. I had no idea what I was doing. All I knew was that I wanted to be near him.

"You brought hamburgers!" He grinned as he opened up the lid.

"Yup. They are fancier than any burger I've ever seen. Look, they even have fancy catsup. Notice how it's spelled with a C?" I pointed to the glass bottle.

Jack laughed and opened the bottle, pouring the red sauce onto his burger. I quickly mimicked him and poured it on my burger as well.

I really liked Jack. I liked the way his smile was slightly crooked, but always genuine when he looked at me. I liked the way he smelled, the combination of cologne and man was intoxicating. I liked that he seemed to relax with me. His shoulders seemed to lower as I watched him poor sauce on his plate for the fries, like he was unwinding.

Jack sat down next to me, our knees barely inches from touching. A current of electricity ran between us and I knew if we touched, sparks would fly. A nervous giggle escaped and I tried to keep it under control. I wanted to be sophisticated and interesting, but I was pretty sure I was nervous and obviously attracted to him.

"Tell me about your day," he said, lifting the lid to one of the entrees.

"You really want to know?" I asked, raising the lid to my own plate. It smelled divine. Jack nodded and took a bite of his dinner. "Well, Dean—my bodyguard—took me to the New York Museum of Art and gave me a tour."

"Dean knows art?" Jack asked, his mouth full of

burger. The normalcy of it made me smile.

"Yeah, a lot about art in fact. I've never really understood what makes one painting better than another, but having him explain the paintings to me actually made it interesting." I took a bite of my own food before asking, "What about you? How was your day?"

"Insane. We had a board meeting today and practically everything is behind or delayed. I don't want to bore you with the details, but this is honestly the best part of my day today. Tell me more about the museum. I haven't gone in years and never with a guide."

"Like I said, I know almost nothing about art, but I did discover I have a favorite artist. Monet. His paintings make me feel like summer. I don't know if that makes sense, but I'm happy when I look at them." I blushed, feeling like I had revealed something.

"Monet... he did the water lilies painting, right?" Jack asked, his brows scrunched together as he tried to remember the artist.

"That's one of the most famous ones. They had one there called, "View of Vétheuil". It reminds me of summers at home. Here I took a picture." I pulled out my ancient flip phone and began navigating through the menus to show him some of the pictures from the museum.

"How old is that phone?" Jack asked, looking askance at the archaic device. I shrugged.

"I'm not really sure. I 'inherited' it when I got my phone plan and I haven't had the money to upgrade it. My plan isn't up for renewal for a while yet." I shrugged sheepishly.

"You are getting a new one. Whatever the top of the line one is right now, I am getting you one," he said, pulling out his own smart phone. He hit a button and held it up to his ear. "Rachel? Emma needs a new phone. All the bells and whistles. Yes. Thank you."

"Thank you," I said as he hung up. I was a little baffled. Despite all the shopping I had done with Rachel, the idea of spending money the way Jack spent money was still intimidating.

"You are most welcome. Let me see the picture." He reached over and took my hand, pulling the phone screen to where he could see it. His hand was hot against mine and it sent sparks racing through my spine. I was a little sad when he let go. "It's beautiful, like you. I can see why you like it."

"Thank you." I couldn't help but smile at the compliment. I wondered if he was this charming to all the models he took to the social events from the tabloid pictures. I hoped it was only for me.

There was a long pause as neither of us knew what to say next. It had been so easy to talk to him on the beach, but now, I was tongue-tied and shy. I played with my food, trying desperately to think of something to say.

"So... , how are you liking New York?" Jack finally asked, breaking our awkward silence.

"It's huge!" I blurted out. Jack laughed. "I mean, it is so much bigger than where I'm from. It's been a little overwhelming."

"Do you think you could get used to it?" There was more to the question than just the words and the implication made my heart speed up.

"If I keep getting to have dinners like this, then I think I could." A smile flashed across Jack's face. It reminded me of a time in high school when I said "Yes" to a boy who asked me for a date—excited and optimistic. It made my chest go tight and my knees loose.

"I'm glad then. I'm glad you're here." Jack set his empty plate on the table and reached over, placing his hand on my knee. A surge of heat splayed out from my belly at his touch. Even though my head wasn't sure what Jack and I were doing, my body knew exactly what it wanted. He leaned forward and our lips hovered inches from one another. I could tell he wanted to kiss me, but something was stopping him. He pulled his mouth away from mine.

"Jack?"

He leaned back, keeping his hand mercifully on my leg. It made it hard to think, but I would have gone crazy if I couldn't have him touching me. My body sang out for more while my head begged for caution.

"I think we should take things slow," he said. His words were controlled and even, but the tightness in his jaw told me that this wasn't easy for him to say. "With the public eye on us, we can't afford any more mistakes."

"*More* mistakes?" my knee pulled away from his hand before I could stop it, and I instantly regretted it when he let me go. I wanted him to touch me and yet I was nervous of what it might lead to. I wasn't sure where we were going. I wished my body would stop pushing for more and for my head to stop worrying.

"I didn't mean it like that," he said holding up his hands in defense. He sighed, "I am the image of my company and we can't afford any bad press right now." He placed my hand in his and he brought it to his lips. "I think you are beautiful and fascinating. I thought so the moment I met you. There is no mistake there, and now, since you're here, I'd like to take the time to get to know you. I mean, really get to know you—not just random secrets and how your body reacts when you're excited. We have time now." His eyes glinted with memories of what I did when I was excited.

"Jack, how long *am* I going to be here?" I asked, looking up into his hazel eyes. They were greener today. A girl could happily drown in those green seas.

"As long as you'd like."

My mouth went dry and I tried to swallow. I hadn't thought about how long I was going to be in New York. It still felt like I was on vacation. None of this seemed like it could possibly be real life. *How long was I going to stay? Another week? A month? A year? Forever?* My breath caught at the idea of forever, though I wasn't sure if I was apprehensive or excited. If we connected half as well in New York as we did on the island, forever might not be long enough.

What about my friends? My family? My job? I was still waiting on responses to my vet school applications. I had already interviewed at several universities and was waiting to hear back on their decisions. I wondered if there was a vet school in New York I could apply to.

My head spun for a second, too many thoughts swirling through it. My only anchor was Jack's hands holding mine. They were warm and real and all I wanted.

"Jack, I don't know what to say. This whole thing has me upside down and I don't know what I'm doing," I whispered. He gripped my hands tighter.

"Neither do I, but I do know that no one makes me feel the way you do. Today was crappy until you walked in that door. I don't know how you manage it, but I'm pretty sure you're magic." Jack's words made me glow.

"You make me feel pretty amazing yourself," I said with a blush. Jack grinned, his smile lighting up the room. He leaned forward, guiding his lips towards mine. It felt so natural, so right as I leaned in.

The phone suddenly rang, jarring the moment to a standstill. Jack swore lightly under his breath, our lips never connecting. He stood, dropping my hand and striding forcefully across the room. His demeanor changed as he picked up the phone. His face was darker, less rounded with happiness and thinner, sterner with strength and power. He was master of his domain... and he knew it.

I played with my empty plate, making designs in the leftover sauce with my fork. I glanced at my watch and saw that our allotted dinner hour was up. It was time for Jack to get back to work. Our mini vacation together was over. I wondered if this was going to be a recurring theme for us, the only time we got to spend together was a few short reprieves from our daily lives. I hoped we could be more.

Jack clicked the phone down on his desk and I stood up and started putting the now empty plates back on the cart.

"Thank you for dinner, Emma," he said softly. I looked up. The boy from the beach was looking at me, his hazel eyes glowing in the light. I wanted to kiss him so badly right then.

"It was my pleasure. I'll have Jeannette put me in your schedule permanently."

Jack took a step forward, closing the distance between us. The room closed in and was suddenly very warm. I felt like a schoolgirl alone with her crush for the first time, my heart pounding wildly in my chest.

"I have wanted to do this all night," Jack whispered, reaching his hand to my chin. He gently guided me to his lips. Fireworks exploded in my brain and I swear a brass band was playing a happy song as he kissed me. I pressed up against him, feeling his strong body mold into mine. His arms wrapped around me, pulling me in closer as his tongue quested for mine.

I could have stood there kissing him for the rest of the evening, but the phone began to ring again. Jack ignored it for a moment, but when the shrill sound refused to stop, he released me. His kisses left me breathless, dizzy and craving more.

"Call back in two minutes," Jack said into the phone. He didn't wait for an answer as he set it down in the receiver.

"What if that was important?" I gasped, tearing my eyes away from his perfect mouth.

"It's always important. If they want to talk to me, they'll call me back. Now where were we?" He stepped forward again, his smile hungry. He was about to reach for me again when the phone began to jingle off its hook yet again.

"I think they want you almost as much as I do," I said, glaring at the offending phone. Jack chuckled. He leaned forward and kissed me softly, our lips barely pressing together, but filling me with desire and the hope for more.

"I look forward to seeing you tomorrow," he whispered, and then turned and stepped behind his wooden desk. The mask of power slipped over his features, turning him cold and indifferent.

I towed the empty food cart out, closing the door carefully behind me. The heavy wooden door blocked the sound of his phone conversation, and I sighed and leaned back against it. That kiss...

Butterflies danced in my stomach. I was giddy and happy, his kiss still lingering on my lips. It was like our first kiss all over again. In a way, it kind of was. It was our first kiss as a real couple, not two strangers on vacation. I wasn't sure what was going to happen next, but all I could see for the future was good things.

CHAPTER FIFTEEN

ஒ௦ ௦௦

I smiled as the golden elevator whisked me up to the top floor of Jack's building. I didn't get to see much of Jack during the day, so the only time I got to spend any time with him was over dinner. After our first dinner, we quickly figured out a routine. The past couple of weeks, I would arrive at his office at a quarter to six and bring dinner with me. We would eat and talk, and usually end up kissing. We never seemed to have time for anything more than intense kissing, as every time we got close to going further, a business emergency would spring up. Jack did his best to clear out an hour of time so that we could eat together, but we were usually interrupted. It was like the phone was an overzealous guardian of our virtue.

I waved to Jeannette as I pushed a trolley full of food towards the big wooden doors. She smiled, her eyes bright and fingers quick on the keyboard despite her gray hair. She was used to our nightly dinners and was always friendly. Jack opened the door to his office, letting me in. His hair was messy, as though he had run his fingers through it one too many times. He looked worn and tired, but his eyes were shining as he smiled at me.

"I don't know how you keep this all straight," I said, waving my hand over the unruly stack of papers covering his desk. He grimaced and grabbed my hand, leading me over to the couch on the far side of his office. The wheeled trolley followed me dutifully with two silver food covers ready to be opened. I pushed the tray so it made a little table in front of the couch for the two of us to eat off before sitting next to him. He made sure I sat close to him, our bodies almost touching but not quite. "What are you working on today?"

"No work for a little bit. You are my break from work." He kissed my cheek, smiled and lifted the tray to reveal a salmon and risotto dish that smelled heavenly. His knee bumped mine and stayed there, pressed against my leg.

"Did you get my picture of that dog today?" I asked, taking a bite of the salmon, but my thoughts entirely on how nice it felt to touch him.

"I nearly spit my coffee across the board of directors," he said with a laugh. "Best part of my day, other than right now."

I grinned and took another bite. Since the camera on my new phone surpassed the abilities of my actual camera by a great deal, I was having a blast taking pictures of things I found in the city. Dean and

Rachel kept me busy during the day, sending me to various well supervised events throughout the area. If something appealed to me, I would take a picture and send it to Jack. At first I thought it might be too silly for a busy man, but he always asked for more. He seemed to live vicariously through the pictures I took throughout the day.

"The woman said it designed by a groomer in Queens who does only specialty cuts."

"If we ever get a dog, can we please never die it blue and give it a lion's mane? Please?" He laughed. My breath caught in my throat for a moment at the implied future. I was about to tease him about possibly going with a tiger striped look instead, but a knock on the door interrupted me.

His secretary poked her head inside, a crisp gray bun at the nape of her neck. "I'm very sorry Mr. Saunders, but Mr. Ryans is calling from Saudia Arabia. He says it is urgent," she said. Jack sighed and set down his meal. There wasn't much left, as he had wolfed it down. My own plate had only been nibbled on.

"Thank you, Jeannette. Tell Owen I'll talk to him in a moment," he said with a sigh. Jeanette nodded and gave me an apologetic smile before closing the door. "I'm sorry to do this to you... *again.*"

"You are very busy. I don't know how you juggle all of the transition details as well as the day to day stuff. I'm just glad I get to see you at all."

"You are too sweet. I have stolen you away from your life and friends, and all I can give you is an hour a day, and not even a guaranteed hour!" He shook his head. I could see guilt weighing down on his broad shoulders.

"Hey, I'm having a great time. Rachel and Dean have been keeping me busy. I saw the Statue of Liberty today. I never thought I was going to see it, let alone have a special tour. I'm finding a routine, and we'll make this work. Rachel is even coming up with a way for me to help you get through all this," I said, motioning to the crazy stacks of papers threatening to overwhelm his desk.

"What is she having you do?" Jack's brows came together as he stood and moved towards the blinking light on his desk.

"I'm not sure yet. I told her I was going to go stir crazy if I didn't have something productive to do. I've been here almost two weeks and I don't want to be a burden. I want to help," I explained as I began to put the dishes back on the tray.

Jack beamed at me. "You are the exact opposite of a burden. I don't know what I would do if I didn't have these evenings to look forward to." The little light flashed faster and he glared at it.

"Will you be coming home tonight or sleeping here again?" I asked as I headed towards the door. I realized he was a busy man, especially right now, and that he often found it easier to spend the night at his office. If he did come back to the apartment, he always came to see me. Two nights before, he even slept in my room. We had intended for more, but he fell asleep as soon as he hit the pillow and I enjoyed watching him sleep. It wasn't much, but I treasured any time I got to spend with him.

"I don't know yet. Depends on how long this takes." He jerked his head towards the angry flashing light. "Don't wait up for me."

"Come wake me up if you do make it back. I have more pictures of that dog to show you."

I pushed the trolley to the door and left, hearing him pick up the phone and switch on the commanding voice he never used with me. I waved goodbye to Jeannette as I headed towards the gold elevators leading back to the main entrance. The older woman waved back as she spoke into her headset. I was quickly becoming accustomed to the silent waves and the smiles over business phone conversations.

Once in the elevator, I hit the button and leaned on the ornate sides. I was having a wonderful time in New York, but some days, I barely understood what I was doing here. These dinner visits were the highlight of my day. I knew Jack and I had a connection, but I wasn't sure if we could ever actually make this work. There wasn't anything for me to do, except spend Jack's money and bother Rachel, and neither of those things were in my nature. I needed something to do.

***

I lay in bed, comfy in my worn PJs, debating opening the newest copy of *The Press* laying on my nightstand. I was emblazoned on the cover, thankfully wearing one of the beautiful outfits Rachel deemed suitable, walking around the city. It had been on one of my recent shopping excursions with Rachel. She wielded a credit card like a magic wand and enjoyed finding things for me to wear. If nothing else, our excursions gave me something to do, and I was forming a friendship with Rachel. I had stopped looking at price tags after the first store rang up my three pairs of pants at more than a month's pay with overtime. Rachel never batted an eyelash at the numbers, letting the purchases pile up in the chauffeured car.

I flipped open the cover, landing on the article about me. Rachel had placed a large sticky note over the first paragraph with the words, "are you sure you want to read this?" I smiled and lifted it off the page. I liked Rachel. She had a subtle sense of humor that caught me off guard. She was fiercely protective of Jack, and the love and respect she had for him only made me like her more. She had grown up in a smaller town than mine, and we spent much of our shopping excursions swapping stories about home. She was quickly becoming the older sister I never had, and I was more than grateful to have her with me in this strange place.

Emma LaRue—the mysterious woman who has stolen the heart of a billionaire! See what her friends and family have to say! exclaimed the headline. The "friends and family" were people I barely knew. My real friends and family had signed confidentiality agreements and weren't speaking to the press without approval. *Emma's best friend from elementary school, Hannah Smithson, remembers her being a shy and studious girl. "I always got along really well with Emma. She was easy to talk to."* Hannah? I hadn't spoken to her since third grade and we were convinced there was a unicorn in the woods behind the school. I shook my head at the lengths the tabloids were going to in order to get a story.

The magazine had a few more pictures, obviously snapped from sidewalks as I hurried out of the winter air into stores. I wondered how cold those photographers had gotten waiting for me to emerge from a store. Spring was on its way, but winter still had an icy grip on the city's weather. The last page of the article had a short note at the bottom: *Do you have any information on Emma LaRue?* The Press *would love to hear your stories! Call to inquire about our payments for photos!* Jack's father's policy of do nothing and keep everyone quiet was working so far, but the entire tone of the article made it clear that readers were clamoring for more. It was a strange feeling.

I set the magazine back on the nightstand and checked my phone. I loved my new phone. I had spent the better part of a day setting it all up and playing with all the games and features, and I still found new and fun things to do with it. I had one unread message from Jack.

I grinned and opened it like it was a present.

Not going to make it home tonight.

Not quite the present I was hoping for. I could feel the pout on my face as the question rose in my mind again. What was I doing here? While I loved my dinners with Jack, my days were full of boredom. Rachel promised to find me a job at the company so that I could at least feel useful, but even then, working for Jack wasn't what I wanted to do with my life. I missed my job at the Vet Clinic, missed working with animals and the people that came with them. For the millionth time that week, I wondered what was going to happen once all the publicity of our pseudo-marriage was finally sorted. I knew Jack had lawyers looking into the validity of the marriage, but we both knew it wouldn't stand up in a court of law. We had never intended it to.

My phone chirped. *I'm going to make it up to you though.*

How?

Tomorrow night. Wear something fancy. I'm taking you to La Maison.

I grinned. La Maison wasn't the fanciest restaurant in New York, but it was pretty close. More important than the fanciness of the restaurant was the significance it held for Jack. La Maison was the restaurant that his father always took his mother for special anniversaries. It was where Daniel proposed to Bianca, so having Jack take me there meant something.

Do I get you all to myself?

I told Jeannette she's fired if she interrupts us tomorrow.

I'll be there with bells on. I typed back. I hit send and turned off the light, snuggling into the soft down comforter. I would have to have Rachel help me pick out something; tomorrow was going to be a great day.

CHAPTER SIXTEEN

I was a princess, a beautiful, only slightly slutty, princess. I smoothed the fabric of my dress over my knees as the car stopped in front of La Maison. The driver hurried out and opened the door, helping me out onto the sidewalk. I saw the people on the street turn and look at me, and was once again glad Rachel had helped me pick out my outfit.

The dress was a fitted black fabric that somehow shone purple in the light and had a slit up my thigh that my father would have considered indecent. It was made by a designer whose name I could barely pronounce, but who Rachel said was the biggest thing in fashion right now. I took a step and wobbled, but the driver reached out a hand to steady me. Rachel had chosen the shoes as well—black strappy stilettos that made me feel as tall as a New York skyscraper, but not quite as stable. Between the slit and the shoes, my legs looked long enough to make swimsuit models jealous.

My hair was piled in effortless looking curls that cascaded down my back. It had taken the hairdresser almost two hours and was anything but effortless. Rachel had procured me a diamond necklace with matching dangling earrings that I couldn't afford if I used every paycheck in my lifetime. The jewelry was gorgeous, but I had this nagging fear that the earrings were going to slip out of my ears, or the chain would break on the necklace and I would lose one of the sparkling stones. I could just see them falling off and bouncing down the street as I scrambled to chase them in my insane heels. The tabloid headlines would be spectacular. As a result, I checked impulsively every minute or two to make sure the jewels hadn't abandoned me.

The restaurant was in a tall brick building from the 1920s. It screamed old money, and it was beautiful. I stepped inside, glad of the warmth in the restaurant. Someone took the simple black wrap Rachel had chosen to complete my ensemble and we headed into the main part of the restaurant.

Every eye in the restaurant followed as the maître d' escorted me to the table where Jack was waiting. I sent a silent, *Thank you,* up to Rachel for making sure that they all saw something fashionable and worthy of a billionaire.

I suddenly understood how Cinderella felt arriving at the ball. Every head in the restaurant turned and watched as I floated gracefully through the tables. For once in my life though, I didn't care that they were looking. The dress gleamed in purple highlights as I approached the only eyes that I cared about. Jack stood as he saw me, his mouth hanging open slightly. Our eyes connected, and I was Cinderella meeting my Prince.

Jack moved to greet me, pulling out my chair and waiting on me like a gentleman. As I approached the table, Jack reached his hand out for mine, to guide me into my chair and I reached back for him. Time slowed, and for a brief second, everything was perfect. I never touched his hand though, as a guest at the next table suddenly pivoted and took my picture.

The flash was blinding and I stumbled in my ridiculous shoes. I caught myself on the back of the chair, lights suddenly flashing from all directions. Jack had the first man's camera in his hands, but more popped up, their flashes lighting up the room like broken lightning.

Cameras were everywhere, the waiters and guests making everything chaotic. There were too many cameras pointed in my direction. I panicked and turned to escape back the way I came, but the flashes were everywhere. I took a step forward, but a light went off directly in my eyes and I ran directly into something hard. Wheeling to catch myself, my shoes betrayed me and I fell to the ground. I came down hard on my wrist, a yelp of pain escaping. The restaurant went quiet except for the clicks and buzzes of cameras.

Suddenly strong arms surrounded me, picking me up and scooping me away. I buried my face into Jack's chest, smelling his cologne, feeling his arms tighten protectively around me as he whisked me away towards the kitchen. His chest vibrated with a growl and I didn't dare remove my face from the protection of his jacket. I could still hear the flashes popping as we disappeared behind the serving door and the startled yells of kitchen staff as Jack barreled through towards the back alley.

He stopped at the back door, the only sounds following us were of the kitchen staff chopping and sautéing. The photographers were yelling at the kitchen door, but security held the door closed. Jack set me down gently, making sure my feet were firmly planted before pulling out his phone and hitting a number.

"In the alley! Now!" he growled before slamming the phone back into his jacket pocket. I kept holding onto him, my fingers clinging to the starched white fabric of his dress shirt. A car peeled into the alley and Jack opened the back door and hurried me out into the blustering winter night, carefully shielding me from the wind as we stepped to the car.

"Are you alright?" He asked once we were in the car, his voice low and gruff. I couldn't see his face in the dimness of the car, but I could hear the anger in his voice. I nodded.

"I think so. I hurt my wrist, but, I think it will be alright," I said as I held onto the offending wrist with my opposite hand. It had a dull ache, but nothing a couple of pain relievers and a night's sleep wouldn't fix.

"Let me see," he said gently. He reached over and took my wrist in his hands. They were so warm compared to the cold outside. He squeezed gently, his fingers searching for any injury.

"You're shaking. Carl, turn up the heat!"

"I forgot my wrap at the restaurant," I said quietly, suddenly remembering I didn't have it. With my free hand, I checked the earrings and necklace to make sure I still had them. I felt a small sigh of relief escape my lungs at finding the jewels still secured to my body. Jack kept running his fingers along the sensitive skin of my inner wrist, making me forget the pain. It didn't hurt anymore, but I didn't take my wrist back from him.

"I'll send someone to fetch it later." His fingers stopped but he held onto my wrist.

"What happened back there anyway?" I asked. I was finally starting to feel warm, the air blowing out of the car heater getting the winter out of the car. I couldn't stop shaking though.

"I made a mistake." His voice was gruff, full of anger under the surface.

"What do you mean? There's no way you could have known those paparazzi were going to be there like that. I mean, they chase me everywhere." I tried to put a smile into my voice, but I knew it was still shaky.

"I have eaten at that restaurant a hundred times. When I made the reservations, I didn't even think about their security. I should have let my security check the place out, but the manager said they had sufficient security for us. I didn't have Rachel do it because I wanted to do this myself." He held my wrist up. "I should have let her set it up. It is my fault you got hurt."

"Jack, it isn't your fault that I'm a klutz and I tripped—"

"No," he said, cutting me off. "This happened because of me. The paparazzi have been after you since the moment they found out about you. I made the reservations and didn't get enough security. This never would have happened if I were anyone else. This could have been much worse. You got hurt because of who I am. This isn't fair to you. I am so sorry Emma." His words never faltered, coming out sure and smooth, but I could hear the guilt threatening to overwhelm him.

"Jack, I don't blame you. This could have happened to anyone."

He carefully placed my wrist back in my lap and then pulled his hands away from me, as though he were afraid he would hurt me again.

"I'm sorry I put you in this position Emma." All I could see was his silhouette in the dark, but his voice was all business. He never used that tone with me.

"Jack, "I started but I didn't know what to say. I didn't know how to talk to the businessman side of him. I fell quiet as the car turned into the parking structure for the penthouse.

Jack slid out and opened the door, helping me out as I tried not to trip over the dress. He let go of my hand as soon as I was free of the car, dropping it like it burned. I stepped towards the elevators, turning to see if he was going to follow, but he climbed back into the car.

"I'm going to have Rachel increase your security

detail. I don't want this happening again." There was a coolness to his voice that I didn't recognize. I stepped back towards the car and tried to smile.

"Will you come up and join me for some dinner upstairs? I think I saw some soup in the kitchen," I tried.

"No. I'm going to go back to work. I think I'll be staying at the office again tonight." He reached for the car door, preparing to close it.

"Oh," I nodded. I ignored the ache growing in my chest. "If you get done early, you know where to find me."

He nodded, avoiding eye contact as he closed the door. I stepped up onto the curb and the car turned and drove away. I couldn't see him through the tinted glass, but I something inside of me cracked. I called the elevator and stepped in alone. What was supposed to have been a beautiful, magical, romantic evening, had turned into something sour, dark... and angry.

CHAPTER SEVENTEEN

An insistent buzzing woke me. I kept my head buried in my pillow and fumbled around on the nightstand trying to find the off switch for my phone. I didn't have to be up yet, and I still felt groggy and disappointed from the night before.

My phone slipped out of my fingers and clattered to the floor, still buzzing like an angry hornet. I thought about leaving it, but someone started pounding on my door. There was no way I was going to be able to sleep through the phone and the knocking on my door.

"It's open," I yelled, rolling onto my back and then throwing my feet off the bed. This was not the way I wanted to be woken up.

"You need to get up. Now," Rachel commanded as she barged into my room. I was about to complain, but the stormy look on her face kept the words inside. She stalked over to my closet and began tossing clothing onto my bed.

"What's going on?" I stood up and stifled a yawn before catching a satin dress shirt with my head.

"The Saunders!" She said it like it was an earthquake or an alien invasion. The finality and doom in her voice, combined with her sudden nervousness, made me go cold. "You need to get up and get dressed right now."

I grabbed the suit she thrust at me and grabbed at the shirt that had fallen around my shoulders and scampered into the bathroom. I hurried through my morning routine, dressing quickly in the expensive dress suit. Rachel had a pair of stylish heels ready for me when I emerged. They were surprisingly comfortable and accented the outfit nicely. I glanced at myself in the full length mirror as Rachel pushed me out the door. Rachel had done a fantastic job shopping for me. I was amazed at how properly fitted clothes instead of baggy sweats actually made me look like a real woman instead of a lumpy sack of potatoes.

I hurried down the hallway after Rachel, trying desperately not to trip in my heels. Despite being fairly low and comfortable, I still felt wobbly on them. Especially after my incident with heels last night, I wasn't keen on any shoe that wasn't a sneaker.

Rachel stopped before the heavy wooden door leading into the main dining room. I rarely went into the dining room, choosing to eat at the more comfortable kitchen table or on the couch in the living room. Rachel turned and straightened my collar, her usually unreadable face pale.

"Address them as 'Ma'am and Sir'. Do not contradict either of them, but especially not Mr. Saunders." The way she said Mr. Saunders made it clear she meant Jack's father. "Be more polite to them than anyone you have ever met in your life. Smile and be pleasant. For the love of God don't tell them you are sleeping with Jack or have ever slept with Jack or even have ever thought of sleeping with him."

I nodded, still confused as to what was going on. "Right, Sir and Ma'am. Be polite."

"Mrs. Saunders is actually the driving force behind the two of them, but it is Mr. Saunders that wields the power in public. Pretend to ask him if you have a question, but it is Mrs. Saunders that you need to suck up to. Got it? Be brave. I'm not even supposed to be here right now, but I couldn't send you into the lion's den without a warning." Rachel smoothed the fabric on my shoulders, and checked my collar one last time before flashing a nervous grin and moving out of the way for me to open the door to the dining room.

I opened the heavy wooden door, unsure of what to expect.

Inside, an attractive elderly couple was sitting across from one another, calmly sipping coffee and eating danish and scrambled eggs. It would have been a normal breakfast scene, if it weren't for the ridiculously expensive clothing, the mahogany table with fine china, and the engraved silverware.

"Good morning, dear," Mrs. Saunders greeted me, setting her coffee cup down delicately on the table. She had short blonde hair swept up into an elegant style and dark brown eyes. Her features were petite, but age had put enough weight on her to make her solid. She still had high cheekbones and a regal manner that made me want to curtsey.

"Good morning. It is a pleasure to meet you both," I said. I was glad my voice didn't quaver despite my nerves.

"So you're the one distracting my son and making him the center of the tabloid gossip," Mr. Saunders said, gesturing to the stack of tabloids and newspapers on the table. The Saunders' name blared out across several headlines, the picture of him carrying me like a child, wrath and concern battling his face. I swallowed hard and nodded.

"Come and have some breakfast, Emma. We have some things to discuss," Mrs. Saunders motioned to an empty chair. I managed to sit down fairly gracefully. I carefully poured a cup of coffee from the carafe on a silver platter. I wished I had something to make it stronger; it felt like I was going to need it.

"Did you marry my son?" Mr. Saunders had waited until I had taken my first sip and set the cup down on the table. He placed his hands on the shiny wooden table and made sure I was looking into his blue eyes. I liked his straightforwardness.

"Not legally. We did have a marriage ceremony, but it was never meant to be anything but a vacation memory. It was never supposed to go this far. It was a spur of the moment decision," I answered honestly. Mr. Saunders continued to evaluate me with his piercing blue eyes.

"Jack told me that you didn't know who he was at that time. Is this true?" Mrs. Saunders asked, sipping delicately on her coffee. Two sets of eyes stared intently at me. I could tell they would know instantly if I was lying or even thinking of lying. I had no intention of telling them anything but the truth. I wanted desperately for his parents to like me.

"Yes, Ma'am. The only time I read the gossip page is when I am waiting in line at the grocery store, and even then I only glance at the covers. They aren't my preferred reading material. I honestly had no idea who he was until I got home and found my face on all these papers."

Mrs. Saunders peered over her cup, appraising me like I was fish at the market. Her eyes weighed and measured me as she inwardly debated whether she wanted to purchase or if I was spoiled goods. My mouth felt dry despite my coffee and I forced myself not to lick my lips.

"Do you love him?" Mrs. Saunders asked, her voice casual. She sounded as though she were simply talking about the weather and not matters of the heart. I was about to give a pretty answer, one that was cautious and what I thought she wanted to hear, but nothing about being with Jack was cautious. I gave the truth.

"Honestly, Ma'am? I'm not sure. I've never been in love before. He makes me feel things that I have never felt in my entire life. Things that make my head dizzy with excitement and my heart pound with fear. When I see him, I feel like everything is going to work out in the end; like the world isn't as horrible or dark as it was before I saw him." I paused and took a short breath, needing to explain myself further. "My parents knew each other for three years before they even started dating. My mom says that it took her years to learn to love him, but one day she looked over and realized that she couldn't live without that man near her. I haven't known Jack for three weeks, let alone three years, but I do know that I don't want to live in a world without him. I don't know if this feeling will last another three weeks, three years, or three decades, but I want to try. He makes me want to try."

Mrs. Saunders' face never changed. She nodded her head to the pile of magazines on the table, their headlines blaring out. "What about the cost? They will always find you and want a piece of you."

"They are just pictures. Eventually they will get bored because I am boring. I'm too normal to be on the cover for very long. Someone else will steal the spotlight, but if that is the price for being with Jack, I'll pay it gladly." A sense of calm washed over me as I realized every word was true. I would put up with a million paparazzi photographers for a minute with Jack.

Mr. and Mrs. Saunders looked at one another, a silent discussion rushing back and forth between them over their cooling eggs.

"I would not use the words 'boring' or 'normal' to describe you, Emma," Mr. Saunders finally said, turning to look at me. Mrs. Saunders sighed.

"That's what makes this so hard. I so wanted to dislike you because it would make telling you this part so much easier."

My heart crept into my throat. This was where they told me he was betrothed, that he had actually been married off as a child, that he had a horrible disease that was going to kill him in a week. The quiet ticking of the grandfather clock in the corner of the room was ominously loud.

Mrs. Saunders set her cup down and reached a hand out to mine. It was a familiar gesture, a way to soothe the sting of bad news. "The marriage may never have been legally binding, but he cannot marry you right now. This is a critical time for our company and business must come first. We can no longer delay the transition."

I followed her eyes to Mr. Saunders. At first glance he seemed strong and solid, but as I looked closer, he was far more worn than I thought. A tiredness that he couldn't fight danced around his limbs, dark circles concealed beneath subtle makeup, a thinness even his tailored suit couldn't hide. There was a lean hunger around his mouth and desperation deep in his blue eyes. I had seen that look many times in the vet's office... he was dying.

The realization must have blatantly crossed my face as Mrs. Saunders patted my hand to grab my attention. She continued, her voice low and controlled.

"We haven't spoken to Jack about this yet. He doesn't know the extent of Daniel's illness and the need for a quick transition," Mrs. Saunders said. The soft way her voice caressed her husband's name made my heart ache. "We need him to focus completely on the company and the transition. Investors are already beginning to worry. He cannot have you as a distraction."

"I didn't realize that I was a distraction," I said, putting a little sass in my voice. "What is it that *you* want me to do?" There was a hollowness in the pit of my stomach that I didn't like. The coffee was growing cold in my cup.

Mrs. Saunders sighed, clearly not a fan of my tone. "Jack was always one to rebel when he felt pushed into something he didn't want to do. We would like the separation to come from you."

"What do you expect me to say to him?" I asked. I didn't want my coffee anymore. I didn't want to have this conversation anymore. Mr. and Mrs. Saunders glanced at one another, a silent conversation slipping through the moment again.

"That's up to you. Tell him you can't see him right now. Tell him you don't love him. Break his heart if necessary, but he needs to focus on taking over the company right now. That is what is most important. Too much is at stake for him to explore his feelings for you."

I looked at her brown eyes and saw a strange collection of emotions—concern and cruelty, heartache and determination, reluctance and sadness. She was accustomed to her wealth and getting what she wanted for her sons. Although she wanted to like me, she obviously thought her son could do better. She wanted her son to be happy, but the company must survive—it was like one of her children. She was being forced to choose between the happiness of two of her children.

I nodded slowly, trying to process exactly what she wanted me to do. She wanted me to leave Jack. I wasn't sure if the request would be simple or the hardest thing in the world. I didn't really care about the company, I only cared about Jack. I wanted to scream "Who the fuck do you think you are?" but I knew that would get me nowhere. I decided it would be better to just let them tell me what they wanted. I could fight it later.

"It is of course your decision. We would never force you, or Jack, into something you don't want to do," Mrs. Saunders said. Her voice was smooth, like a salesman's.

I wanted to say *'You are currently forcing Jack'* but I bit my tongue.

She sighed. "One last thing. This may help you decide. This came in the mail to your house. We had it forwarded here."

She slid a large envelope with a fancy seal across the table. It was from my first choice of vet schools. I picked it up with shaking hands, the size of the envelope promising admission. I noticed there was a normal sized envelope bearing the DS Oil and Gas logo attached with a paperclip.

"You've been accepted to the school. We had nothing to do with your admission, but there is a full scholarship set up in your name if you take it and leave our son to run his business. Included is a sizable sum to help you cover any expenses." Mrs. Saunders paused as I weighed the two envelopes in my hands. "If you stay with Jack, you can never become a vet. People would line up with their dogs and cats to become your clients and patients because they know if you make even the slightest mistake, they can sue you for millions. You will never be able to practice without the fear that they were using you. If you stay with Jack, you become part of the company—an employee like the rest of us. You will be lost in a world that is not of your making. Dinners and charities will fill your days instead of animals. Your dreams will die."

I set the two envelopes down in front of me, the DS Oil and Gas logo merging with the seal on the acceptance envelope. Mrs. Saunders watched me, her eyes cold. I wondered what she had given up to be be where she was now. I hoped this was her way of preventing what happened to her happen to me. I felt light headed. I couldn't decide if I was angry, confused, frightened or grateful.

"So,... you're bribing me?" I asked, looking her in the eye. She shrugged.

"If that is how you want to look at it. I prefer it to be a generous parting gift. You made my son smile. You gave him something that money can't buy and this is the only way I know how to repay you. I am giving you an option I never had." *The only way she knows—money for emotions.* I pitied her.

I looked down at the envelopes again. This is what I had wanted for so long. On top of that it would all be paid for. I could have my dream and not go into debt, start my own practice the minute I finish school. I could live the life I had always dreamed of and go back to doing the work I love. Back to my home where people don't push and shove and take pictures for money.

I picked up the two envelopes, stacking them

neatly before holding them out for Mrs. Saunders to take back. *I don't want their money. I want Jack.*

"Think it over for a little while," she said gently, pushing them back towards me. "This money is very little to us, but to you, it would mean your whole future. Take it, and think it over for a day. I know you will make the right decision."

I set the envelopes down on the table, suddenly tired. "I'll think about it then. I can't make any promises though."

"That is all we ask," Mrs. Saunders said with a nod. She smiled. "Would you care for some breakfast?"

"No, thank you. I am afraid I don't have much of an appetite right now. I have some thinking I need to do. Please excuse me." I picked up the envelopes, carefully placing one inside the other, the chair nosily scraping the floor as I stood. The Saunders nodded politely and resumed their breakfast as though they hadn't asked me to choose between my dreams and love.

I managed to make it to the hallway before I started running.

***

I nearly slammed the door to my bedroom, but managed not to. Every nerve in my body was shaking from my encounter with the Saunders. I looked at my freshly made bed and hoped I was going to wake up soon. This had to be a dream.

I placed the envelope on my dresser, trying to

ignore them while I checked my phone. No new messages. It was still early though and Jack always tried not to wake me up. I fell back onto the big bed, feeling the soft bedding catch my fall. I tried to take a deep breath, hold it, and let it out. It didn't work. I still felt flustered and discombobulated.

The envelope stared at me like a judgmental eye. The dolphin necklace that Jack had bought me sat curled up neatly beside it. Two different decisions. Two different paths. I closed my eyes, but I could still feel them there, haunting me to choose. Dreams or Jack?

I let out a frustrated noise and stood up. Lying in bed wasn't going to help me choose. I needed something to do, something productive. I hated sitting around with nothing to do but wait for my dinner with Jack or for Rachel to come entertain me. I hung the dress coat in the closet, smoothed the expensive silk of my shirt, and opened the door to the hallway.

I got two steps before I realized that the Saunders would probably still be eating breakfast in the dining room. They were the last people in the world I wanted to see, so I snuck carefully down the hall past the door to the kitchen. The lights were off and it was empty. A pale cold light through the window sparkled on the stainless steel appliances, but what caught my eye were the roses.

Sitting on the light wooden table was a beautiful bouquet of long stemmed red roses. They smelled divine, their sweet scent filling the kitchen with images of summer. A small card sat next to them, inscribed simply with "For a beautiful lady." It was Jack's messy scrawl. I could barely read it, but it made my heart melt a little, knowing that this was Jack's way of trying to apologize for last night.

I held a flower up and took a deep breath. The scent relaxed me, my shoulders dropping down from my ears to rest where they were supposed to. I picked my phone out of my pocket.

Thank you for the flowers. I love them!

It only took a moment for the reply: *You deserve them. I'm sorry about last night. Do over?*

An idea formed quickly. I could feel a grin spreading over my face as it began to take shape, the pieces falling together.

Dinner is on me tonight. I'll arrange everything.

I took another deep inhale of the flowers. I would need Rachel's help, but I could make this a wonderful evening. It was something that would keep me busy, and give me something to do other than think about the decision sitting on my dresser.

❧ ❧

CHAPTER EIGHTEEN

I sat on the vinyl seat, a nervousness making my hands twitchy. I played with the silverware, the menus, the dinky plastic cup filled with soda. I probably shouldn't have had two full glasses already, but I was nervous and kept refilling it.

I glanced around the small diner. It was nothing fancy—a greasy spoon hamburger joint that reminded me of home. With Rachel's help, I had rented the entire restaurant for the evening. The owner was more than happy to "sell" me the space for an evening, and I had a feeling Rachel was generous with the payment in return for a signed agreement not to tell anyone. No crazy photographers were going to ruin this date night.

I glanced up as the door chimed. Jack walked in the door, wearing a $10,000 suit. I was wearing jeans and a t-shirt—granted it was an Rachel-chosen jeans and t-shirt costing more than a week's salary. I watched as the two bodyguards closed the door behind him. The taxi he arrived in pulled away, immediately lost to a sea of matching yellow cars. The taxi for him, while Rachel drove around in the fancy chauffeured car to keep the paparazzi from following him had been my idea.

"You did all this?" He asked, glancing around the small diner. He looked so out of place as he hung his fancy suit jacket on a coat rack covered with grease, and slid into the seat across from me.

"I thought we could be normal tonight," I said with a smile. He glanced around.

"Where are the other diners?"

"Okay, sort of normal. I bought the restaurant for the evening. The chef and the waitress too. I mean—I didn't buy them—you can't buy people—"

Jack reached out and took my hand, cutting off my nervous chatter. His hand was warm and strong on mine, current flowing through it and sending my already racing heart into a new pattern.

"This is fantastic, Emma. Thank you." His smile made my poor heart do back flips.

An excited waitress bounced over to our booth, her grin nearly pulling her face apart.

"So, what can I get you folks?" She tried to say it normally, but the grin on her face at serving the famous Jack Saunders, gave her excitement away.

Jack didn't even bother opening the menu before ordering.

"I'll take your largest burger with pepper jack

cheese. Can you put a fried egg on it? Perfect. The works on the burger, fries, and a chocolate shake please."

The young girl smiled as she scribbled his order on her pad before turning to me. Her smile seemed to grow even wider as she took my order.

"I'll have the number 2 cheeseburger with everything, an order of half fries half onion rings, and a banana shake. Thank you," I said. The girl beamed at the two of us, obviously star struck. It felt odd to have someone think I qualified as a celebrity. I knew she was trying her best to pretend like we were a normal couple, Rachel was certainly paying her enough, but her smile was infectious. She grinned and hurried off to the kitchen to start our orders.

"How did you do all this?" Jack asked, settling into the red vinyl seat.

"Rachel helped... a lot. I came up with the idea, and she made it happen." I shrugged and smiled. "I wanted us to have a normal date night. You seem exhausted by the billionaire stuff."

A tiredness crossed his face. It was the look I saw disappear when I brought him dinner each night. It passed quickly as he shrugged it off.

"Work is insane. So much has to be done, and the deadlines keep creeping up. I don't want to talk about it. This is a normal date night. Let's talk about something normal."

I laughed a little. Here was a man sitting a suit worth half my year's salary, in a greasy hamburger joint, wanting to talk about normal.

"Well, the Iowa Cubs are looking good this season.

"

Jack cocked his head, obviously confused.

"Baseball. Spring training. They're a feeder team for the Chicago Cubs. They are the closest thing we have to a major league sports team in Iowa. Other than the college stuff."

"I played baseball as a kid. I was never very good," Jack said. He laughed and I loved the sound. For a moment, we were normal. This was how a date was supposed go—sports, weather, laughing and sharing stories. He was the laughing happy man that I met on vacation; the cold business man was gone.

The waitress reappeared with our food, still smiling from ear to ear. Jack chowed down on his burger like it was the only food he had seen all day. Knowing his work schedule, it probably was. I dug into my burger, feeling ketchup drip out onto my plate. Jack swiped an onion ring from my plate, and I snatched one of his fries. This of course led to a fry battle, with the two of us creating elaborate defenses with our food to keep the other from stealing it.

My ribs ached from laughing. Jack's foot kept playing with mine under the table as we played elaborate fry games above. It was a piece of heaven and we hadn't even had pie yet. I was glad we were the only patrons in the restaurant, because we would have been kicked out for acting like rowdy kids otherwise.

I snagged one of his fries as he snuck an onion ring off my plate, making me laugh. The table vibrated, and my fry defense quickly fell. Jack glared at the phone on the edge of the table. It had remained mercifully silent, but now was vibrating as though full of bees. He shot me an apologetic look before reaching for it and standing up.

"I told you no interruptions," he growled into the phone. He was instantly the cold domineering man. I wondered how he could switch on the businessman so quickly. I sighed quietly and leaned back against the booth, as he stalked over to the window, his voice angry.

For ten minutes I played with the straw in my milkshake. The fries were now soggy and the onion rings had lost their magic. I wondered if this would be what my life would be like. Small stolen moments with the laughing young man on the beach, surrounded by an ocean of business calls and interruptions. Would it be worth it?

"I'm sorry Emma," Jack said quietly, taking his seat once again. I sat up once again in my chair.

"Don't be. This is your job, Jack." I smiled, trying to take the sting out of my words.

"It isn't fair to you though. I still have a few minutes before they are coming to get me for an emergency meeting. What kind of pie do you think they have?"

I smiled and handed him a menu. He flashed me a grin that made my insides go mushy. Those eyes could make a girl go crazy. How was I going to decide?

CHAPTER NINETEEN

My laptop screen glowed an eerie blue, casting strange shadows on the walls and window shades. It was well after midnight, but I couldn't sleep, so I was up playing on my computer. I swung my legs as I sat at the big oak desk in the corner of the room. My older sister Kaylee, was online and we were emailing back and forth as I roamed the web in search of anything to take my mind off the envelopes and necklace still watching me from my dresser. I hadn't touched them since I came back from my meeting with the Saunders.

Hey,

Your boss is curious if you are ever coming back to work. They miss you. Dr. Georges says you're his favorite vet tech. His practice has been going through the roof with all your stardom. By the way, there are at least four reporters parked outside your apartment building right now. Mrs. Jenkins calls the cops on them at least twice a day, but they keep coming back. I think she might actually get tired of calling the cops... nah, not her. They actually had to up security at my hospital because photographers kept trying to sneak in and take pictures of me. My boss was pissed.

Mom and Dad are thrilled hat you are seeing someone. They were kind of worried for a while there that they were never going to get any grand kids out of either of us. What is going to happen next? Are you ever going to come home?

-Kaylee

I stared at the screen asking myself the same question. Was I going to go home? Right now I was in limbo, not really belonging in Iowa or New York. I couldn't go back to Iowa with paparazzi staking out my home; though the idea of Mrs. Jenkins calling the cops on them made me smile. At least someone was having a good time because of photographers. I didn't belong here in New York though either. There was nothing for me to do here, nothing productive at least. Rachel made sure I had a daily allowance and access to the company car, but there was no way I was driving in New York City and it didn't feel right taking the money. I hadn't earned it, and I had no real right to any of it.

I hit reply.

Hey yourself,

I'm not sure when I'll be coming back. If there are reporters staking out my house, there is no way I can go home for a while. You know how I forget to close the drapes. That does not need to be on a magazine. I actually have a decision to make soon though.

I got accepted to vet school. My top choice and everything, but going would mean leaving Jack. His parents made it pretty clear that I can't be a vet and stay with him. (Yeah, met his parents. Imagine rich people. That's them to the letter.) I want to stay, but at the same time, this isn't my world. I feel so out of place here. You know me—I'd be happy up to my elbows in a cow and the only thing here is pampered froufrou dogs.

I really have feelings for Jack though. He makes everything better. I am falling for him hard and it feels so good. I think I was waiting to fall in love until I met him.

I have no idea what to do. If you have any ideas, I am all ears, but for right now I am going with the flow. I don't know what is going to happen next, but I'll let you know.

-Emma

I hit *Send* and switched to another page. A recipe on double double chocolate fudge brownies. I would have to ask Rachel to take me to the grocery store later. Maybe I could even find the makings of a dinner and treat Jack to a homemade Iowa dinner.

My inbox beeped and I flipped back. Kaylee had written me back almost immediately.

Heya,

Congrats on the vet school! I know that you have always wanted that.

I don't know what to tell you about the other stuff. I'll write down some ideas and mail them to you in the morning. It's a sticky situation for sure.

Remember your trophy wife ambitions? Who could have seen that coming? Congratulations on following all of your childhood dreams!

-K

I snorted and giggled as I read her message. When I was five I told my dad I wanted to be a trophy wife when I grew up. I thought it meant someone who the trophies were modeled after. I wanted to be the figure kicking the soccer ball on all the soccer trophies. I thought that would be the coolest job ever. My dad laughed so hard he was in tears, but I didn't care. I wanted to be a trophy, and I wanted to be married someday, so that would make me a trophy wife.

I flipped back to my brownie screen. I wondered if Jack liked brownies, and I resisted the urge to look it up. Just because it was probably on a fan site somewhere didn't mean that I couldn't ask him myself.

A soft knock on the door drew my attention. "It's open," I called out. I felt my heart speed up. Security wouldn't let anyone but Jack in here, and the thought of him always made my pulse race.

Jack's sandy head peeked in the door. "I saw the light under the door. Why aren't you sleeping?"

"I have nothing I have to do tomorrow. Why aren't you sleeping?" I grinned at him.

"I came here to watch you sleep. You look so peaceful when you sleep—calm and sure in your world." He closed the door softly behind him as if we would wake the invisible people in the house.

"You watch me sleep? I'm not sure if I should be flattered or creeped-out."

"I prefer flattered," he said softly as he came around to the desk chair. He sat down behind me and put his big hands on my shoulders. The heat in his hands melted away tension I didn't even know was there as he began massaging gently. I closed laptop and leaned back into him, closing my eyes and losing myself to his touch.

I could practically hear the ocean again. Jack had an amazing ability to be able to find every tense or sore spot on my body and make it melt away. I remembered when we had spent a wonderful afternoon on the beach, his hands finding every ache, and then making new ones. His touch ignited a fire, a heat starting to grow between my legs. I had missed him in more ways than one.

Jack leaned forward and kissed my hair. I could hear him breathe in the smell of my hair. A tingle ran through my body, a shiver that wasn't from the cold. I wanted him... badly.

I turned and leaned up to kiss him. It was as if we were instantly transported back in time, back to our little house on the beach. Our time apart melted away as though it had never been. His hands went to the sides of my face, embracing me as he kissed me. It was the tender kiss of two people in love. Soon, however, the kiss turned from tender to passionate, as our tongues began to move against each other. I stood and wrapped my arms around the back of his neck, and his hands went to my sides.

He broke from the kiss. "Would you mind if I stay the night? I think there might be a spider in my room."

I laughed. "That's the oldest trick in the book."

He kept up his poker face. "No, I'm serious. I saw seven, maybe eight legs dart under my bed. It'll keep me up all night."

I smiled, leaning in for another kiss. "Careful," I said, our lips still touching. "I might keep you up all night instead."

"I'd like that," he said. His hands went for my t-shirt, pulling it up. I lifted my arms up and let him take it off me. He had been so busy lately, I had craved his touch. I wasn't about to pass up this opportunity. While he threw it on the floor, I reached behind me and unclasped my bra. As it fell to the floor, my breasts were freed and Jack looked at them hungrily. I smiled. I always smiled at his attention.

He leaned down and took my boobs in his hands, then buried his face in my cleavage. His tongue felt fantastic against my skin, and I grabbed the back of his head and ran my fingers through his hair. I could hear him giving little moans of delight, as if he were eating a delicious snack.

He backed away from me and took off his shirt. He fished around in his pocket for a moment, pulling out a square package. "I hope this isn't being too presumptuous," he said, a wry grin on his face. He tossed me the condom.

I smiled. "You know, most married couples don't even use these, but I appreciate it." I watched as he took his shorts and boxers off, standing fully naked in front of me. I licked my lips, enjoying his taut body. I got on my knees in front of him, opening the condom wrapper as I looked up at him. He was already fully erect, but I decided to make sure. I took him in my mouth, sucking gently for a few seconds. He hissed as if in pain, but bliss radiated from his face. I knew that was what he did when he felt intense pleasure.

In a few moments, I stopped sucking on him and unrolled the condom onto him. I stood up and pulled my shorts off, getting completely naked myself. As I moved closer to him to kiss him, I reached down and grabbed the base of his hot, silky length and slowly began jerking him off. He moved his hands softly across my back, then reached down to one of my legs and pulled it upward, setting it back down on the bed. I guided his throbbing member to my opening. I could feel myself open to him, feel his gentle advances preparing me for his entrance. I wanted him. I needed him.

He inserted himself an inch, then another, then another. The two of us locked eyes as his knees bent and he pushed even farther into me. I wrapped my hands around the back of his neck to steady myself while he wrapped his arms around my waist. Soon, he was pounding into me, filling me with every inch of himself.

The two of us locked eyes and he pulled me close, kissing me. I was on Cloud Nine, making love to this powerful man. He had me right where he wanted me. I was wrapped around his little finger, while my sweet womanhood was wrapped around his solid manhood. This was heaven, I was sure of it.

He pulled out, but kept me where I was at. He walked around behind me, and slowly put his hand on my back. I bent over, exposing myself to him. I knew that he liked the way my ass looked, and he took a moment to rub his hands all over it. Then, he bent down, and entered from behind.

I gasped. He felt gigantic, and his thrusts were immediate and quick. His hands ran all over my back, reading the Braille of my body. I began to cry out as he seemed to grow even larger, plunging deeper into my body.

I could hear him breathing hard behind me, could feel the sweat drip from his forehead onto my back. His hand reached around and grabbed my breast, teasing my nipple into a tight nub of pleasure. His other hand was on my hip, guiding me, showing me exactly what he wanted. He was strong, and I never wanted those hands to let me go.

He pulled out of me, and sat on the edge of the bed. I knelt on the bed on top of him, and lowered myself to meet him. The two of us merged together, his every movement reminding me of how much I wanted him to be a part of me. His hands held onto my ass as he rubbed his face in my chest. I could feel him getting worked up. I sensed that he was reveling in this moment, yet there was no way he was enjoying it as much as I was.

He looked up at me, and we shared another heart-stopping kiss. He put his hand on my back and rolled me towards him. He fell out of me and I giggled and leaned in for another kiss. He broke the kiss and moved his lips to my ear. "Get comfortable," he commanded.

I wiggled up to the head of the bed, putting a pillow under my head. He was on top of me in an instant, slipping into me as though he had never left. I moaned again, admiring the his perfect physique.

I grabbed onto his taut ass with my fingernails, drawing him in deeper. He began to thrust quicker, grunting as he did so. I knew he was close, so I closed my eyes and enjoyed these last few moments, our passion rising in tandem. With powerful thrusts, he filled me completely, then thrust deep and stayed there. A hot fire burned through my core, letting me join him in a perfect moment. A last groan of contentment escaped him, then a few shallow, slow thrusts. He collapsed into me, his face next to my ear, his breathing uneven and heavy.

"You should probably take care of the condom," I said once I was able speak. He groaned as if he wanted to fall asleep there. "Come on, you don't want to make a mess."

"Yes I do," his words muffled by the sheets.

"Get up, lazybones."

He rolled over and pulled the condom off. He tied it in a knot and aimed for the waste basket across the room. He shot... and missed again. Without even looking to see where it landed, he snuggled back up against me. I sighed knowing I would pick it up in the morning. He wasn't perfect, but I loved loved him.

CHAPTER TWENTY

I lay there, wrapped in Jack's arms. They were strong, and I felt safe and warm for the first time since arriving in New York. This is where I was supposed to be... with Jack. When I was with him, everything somehow looked like it could make sense. I glanced over at my nightstand, the envelopes still eying me and the necklace sparkling in the moonlight. I was going to choose Jack.

Jack grunted softly as he released me, the bed suddenly overly warm with our body heat. The bed shifted slightly as he stood and stretched, his muscles glistening in the pale moonlight streaming through the open drapes. I wanted to run my hands up and down his naked body, to touch him and never stop.

He caught my eyes and smiled at the look of hunger. With a grin he turned and walked into the big bathroom, turning on the light. It reflected off the curve of his perfectly sculpted ass and I had to bite my lip in order to keep from drooling. I was a lucky, lucky girl.

I rolled out of the big bed, still unsteady on my feet from the attention he had given my body. The floor was cold under my feet, the tile cold but I didn't care. Jack stood under the spray of the shower, steam filling the room. It reminded me of our vacation and I could feel my body heating again. I was going to be sore in the morning at this rate.

I stepped under the steaming water, feeling the sweat rinse from my skin. Jack stepped into the spray, his body blocking most of it as he wrapped his arms around me. I held this moment in my mind, the heat of the water, the touch of his skin against mine, the scent of him filling my mind. This is what heaven was supposed to be—warm, wet and wonderful.

Jack made a throaty noise and I felt his hands go to my hair. He carefully rubbed shampoo, trying not to tangle my hair but unsure of what he was doing. I could sense the honesty of his actions, the desire only to please even though this was not something he was used to. I closed my eyes and let him massage my scalp, the hot water and his careful fingers removing any tension I might have had.

The fingers stopped and I leaned into the hot water, the scent of my shampoo filling the room. Shampoo foam seemed to keep pouring from my head and I wondered how much he had used. I kept rinsing, the suds pouring down my body in waves.

"How much did you use?" I asked, stepping out of the water for a moment, trying to decide if the lather was gone. It wasn't. I stepped back under.

"I wasn't sure, so a handful."

I ran my fingers through my hair, finally finding the hair instead of soap. Jack held out his big hand like a cup, and I knew how much soap he had used. He had an earnest look on his face, like a child hoping he had done well. It made me smile and adore him even more.

"Um, a quarter of that would have been enough," I said. I rinsed the last suds out, and grinned up at him. "You did well though. Your turn."

Jack dipped his head under the water, spraying small water droplets everywhere as he ran his fingers through his hair. He bent his head towards me so I could reach his sandy colored hair. It was soft beneath my fingers, thick and luxurious. He made a soft noise of pleasure as I worked my fingers into his scalp, the soapy water dripping down his forehead.

He stepped under the faucet again, water and soap running in rivulets down his muscled body. I reached out a finger and traced one, his skin sliding beneath my touch. I could see him harden, his body responding to my touch. A rush of power filled me, but he held still, letting me caress him.

His body was strong. I could feel tension in his shoulders though, tightness across his back from the strain of holding his father's company on his shoulders. I pushed my fingers into his muscles, feeling not only the strength of his body, but the hardness of his stress. He groaned slightly as I increased pressure, letting my fingers find the sore spots as the hot water relaxed him. Jack leaned into my hands, letting me work the ache from his body.

Slowly, his back turned from rock into supple muscle. His shoulders no longer held a hunch, and his face was as relaxed and happy as it had been when we were married. He kissed me softly, an appreciative, *Thank you,* in the simple gesture.

"Are you ready to get out?" The office was out of his voice, but he still sounded tired. This transition was not going as smoothly as either of us could have wished.

"I need to put conditioner in my hair, or I'll never get it brushed," I answered. He kissed the tip of my nose and stepped through the big glass doors. I watched him dry off. The steam obscured the glass, but I could still see enough of his body to make the small flame in my midsection dance and burn.

He finished drying, carefully hanging the towel back on the rack. "Do you mind if I use your computer?"

"Not at all. I'll be out in a minute. The password is 'vacation'."

"Vacation, huh?" I could hear the smile in his voice as he knew it was a reference to him. He closed the door behind him as he left, letting me keep the steam in the shower. It only took me a moment to massage the conditioner into my hair and run my fingers through the tangled tresses. Jack washing my hair had felt spectacular, but the tangles it left behind did not.

I stepped out of the shower and dried quickly, ready to be next to Jack again. I grabbed a fuzzy robe from a hanger and stepped into the bedroom, ready to cuddle. The cold air hit me, but it was Jack's face that made me stop.

He was standing in the middle of the room, his hair still wet and wearing only a pair of pajama pants. Every taut muscle in his chest gleamed as he radiated anger. In his fist was the envelope containing the scholarship information and money offered by his parents; behind him, my laptop screen was open to the email from Kaylee.

"What is this?" The question came out as a growl, his voice low.

I looked at the envelopes. His knuckles were almost white around them. "Your parents offered that to me. They want me to leave you so you can run the company without distraction."

His hand tightened further around the crumpled paper. He took a menacing step forward, eyes blazing. "What about the email?"

"You read my email?" I took a step back, not understanding his anger at the situation.

"It was open when I turned on the computer. I didn't mean to read it, but I'm glad I did. You wanted to bag a billionaire. That's all I am to you. A meal ticket."

A flash of anger surged through me, first that he had read a private message and then at how badly he had misinterpreted it, but the fury directed at me startled me. "It's not like that. You're taking things completely out of context-"

"*Remember your trophy wife ambitions?* How else should I take it?" He spoke in the controlling businessman's voice that broke my heart. He never spoke to me in that voice.

"We were kids and I didn't understand the meaning of the expression! If I had wanted to marry a billionaire, I'm sure there are easier ways!" I didn't mean to yell, but it came out angry. I didn't appreciate his accusations. This was never my plan.

He nodded, a sneer across his usually handsome face. He didn't believe me. He shook his head and held out the crumpled envelopes. "When were you going to tell me?"

"I did tell you—your parents offered me that—"

"They offered you acceptance to vet school?" His voice dripped with scorn.

"What? No, they offered the scholarship. I only just found out." I hated the way my throat was tightening up, the tears slowly gathering at his unjustified anger.

"Right. You wanted me so I could pay for your dream," he spat out the words. I opened my mouth, but he ran right over me. "You made me fall in love with you, but it was all a lie. You never wanted me."

"Jack, that's not true! I was planning on telling you—"

"You were planning on telling me. How nice of you." He glared at me, his eyes dark. His voice was full of venom. "You used me. All you ever wanted was money. I thought you were different, but you are just like everybody else."

My temper finally snapped. I stepped up to him, feeling like lightning should be flashing from my eyes. "How dare you! I never expected this! I never asked for this! You aren't listening to me at all!"

"I don't need to listen to someone like you." He leered at me, his lips in a cruel curve. "Did you pay the guy on the beach so you could be a hero? Was that your plan to catch my attention?"

"You are being paranoid and self-absorbed. I didn't plan anything. This never had anything to do with money. Will you please listen to me?" I pleaded. I didn't like where this conversation was headed.

"Why should I listen to you? You only wanted me for my money. You don't deserve me. "

His words hit me like a slap across the face. Self doubt flooded through me. *I wasn't good enough. Someone like Jack would never be with someone like me. This was all a lie.* I stumbled back, reeling as though I had been physically hit. He sneered and stepped towards me, his face sharp in the moonlight. This was not the man who had snuck into my bedroom only a few hours ago.

I stumbled back into my dresser, trying to escape his hurtful words. My elbow banged the corner, sending a jolt of pain shrieking through my arm.

"Get out of my room," I yelled, the pain making me bold.

"It's my house," he scoffed.

"Get out of my room," I enunciated every syllable clearly, anger vibrating through me. He snickered in the dark. Fury pumped through my veins. I wanted to hurt him like he hurt me."You want me to take your money and run? Then I will do exactly what you want me to do. I was going to give up my dreams for you. You're right. I don't deserve you. I deserve better."

Jack went silent. I was both grateful and

disappointed I couldn't see his face in the dark. I knew my words were hitting home and I didn't care if they were cruel. I reached out and ripped the envelopes from his hand. "I was going to give this back, but since you obviously don't want me, then I will go back to where I belong."

"Emma," he started, the tone of his voice shifting. I was past furious now. The room took on a scarlet haze, every nerve shaking as I cut him off.

"You wanted to push me away. You saw one thing that you didn't like, and instead of trusting me, you accuse me. You wanted to hurt me. Go back to your perfect life in a perfect office, where you don't feel anything or trust anyone. Where you don't have to be vulnerable or even human. Congratulations. You'll get it all back. I'll leave you and your precious money. I know better than to stay where I'm not wanted."

I knew I touched a nerve. I could feel him vibrating as he swore and stormed to the door. The room shook as he slammed the heavy door shut, his footsteps stomping loudly down the hall. The air felt thick and hard to breathe. Everything was suddenly too warm and I felt sticky. I thought I might be sick as my legs crumpled beneath me and I fell to the floor.

The hurt in my heart fueled a fire of anger, the pain masquerading as rage. I knew my words had hit their target. I had hurt him. My arrows had slipped past his carefully constructed armor and gone straight to his heart. It felt like a betrayal, but I was angry enough that I didn't care.

CHAPTER TWENTY-ONE

The small plane landed with a thud, shaking me loose from my thoughts. I replayed our fight over and over again in my head, trying to figure out what had happened. I couldn't understand why he thought I was trying to use him. I had wanted to choose him! Thinking about it made my whole body ache. The plane stopped smoothly at the terminal, and the businessman sitting next to me stood up and left without a word. I didn't mind. I wasn't exactly in a making friends mood.

The plane slowly emptied and I stood up. The short blonde hair on my wig felt strange against my chin, but Rachel had promised me it looked natural. I kept wanting to tug at it, but I didn't want anyone to recognize me. The stewardess smiled politely as I exited the plane, her eyes looking past me at the empty plane. I could tell she was already cleaning it in her mind so she could return to New York. I didn't even try to smile back.

The small airport was empty and I said a silent, *Thank you*. I didn't want to face the paparazzi reporters today, I didn't have the energy. Rachel had found a small charter flight with a seat available. I had snuck through the airport and boarded quietly, hoping no one would notice me. No one did. I spent the flight staring out the window and trying not to annoy the passenger next to me with my sighs.

I had stayed two more nights in New York, hoping that Jack and I would make up. He chose to sleep at his office and wouldn't answer my calls. It had been a long two days by myself. Rachel found me the second day sitting at the kitchen table in tears, surrounded by the dying roses he had sent me. They had all wilted and the similarity to our relationship had been too much.

"I'm going to call him up right now, and tell him exactly what I think," Rachel had said when I finally stopped sniffling enough to tell her what happened. She seemed shocked. "The happiest I have seen him in years is with you, and then he goes and does this... ?"

Her anger at Jack eased the pain a little. It was like cool water on a sunburn—too little to stop the pain, but enough relief to make it better for a moment. She had picked up her cell phone and dialed him right then, full of righteous indignation.

"Jack, I'm with Emma, and—" she started out with strength, but suddenly paled as his voice carried through the phone. It was angry and full of the confidence of a businessman. She stepped away, speaking into the phone with far less forcefulness than she started with. In a matter of moments, she was replying with a meek "'Yes, Sir. No, I understand, Sir. I will see to it, Sir."

She sat down, setting the phone with a quiet tap on the wooden table. She stared at it like it might turn and bite her at any moment.

"Thank you for trying," I said quietly. I knew then that it was time for me to leave.

"I'm sorry Emma. I don't like this at all."

"We're from different worlds. I'm not Cinderella, and you aren't a fairy godmother. Some things aren't meant to be." The words came out with a sad surety. I should have seen this coming. A billionaire and the broke girl from Small Town, Nowhere? That was never going to happen. It had been foolish to think it would. "Will you help me arrange things so I can go home? I'm tired and I want to go back to the way things are supposed to be."

Rachel frowned and then looked up. She looked for a moment like she was going to try and persuade me otherwise, but she glanced at her phone again and sighed. She nodded and stood up slowly. "I'll take care of everything. You go and pack."

Everything had gone quickly from there. Rachel was the only one to see me off at the airport, dropping me off in a nondescript car. I had tried not to cry as she hugged me goodbye, but I was going to miss her can-do attitude and easy smile. I wondered as the car had pulled away if she was going to tell Jack I was gone. I still hadn't heard from him since our fight, despite leaving him multiple messages.

"Miss Street? Miss Anna Street?" A light masculine voice cut through my memories. A tall older gentleman, with combed back brown hair sliced with gray and bright blue eyes was trying to catch my attention. I suddenly recognized Dean, though it took me a moment before I remembered that I was traveling as Anna Street to avoid alerting any of the press. I rushed over and hugged him, glad to have a familiar face when my world seemed so empty. He grinned and hugged me back before tucking the sign with my false name printed neatly across it under his arm and ushering me to a waiting black SUV.

"Looks like you made it here safe and sound. Rachel hired me to look out for you for the next few weeks. She thought it was best if it was someone you knew and trusted already." I was so glad it was Dean who was going to look out for me. Just hearing his voice was soothing. It was like he was always smiling, even though his face was straight and professional. He reminded me so much of my father it was easy to trust him.

"I'm glad you're here Dean. Where are we going?"

"Ms. Weber has arranged for you to stay at a local hotel."

"A hotel? You mean I don't get to go home?" I felt a push of despair. All I wanted was to curl up in *my* bed, in *my* house, with *my* special coffee mug and try to forget this whole thing had ever even happened.

"I'm sorry, but no. There are at least three photographers waiting at your home and several more positioned at places that you are known to frequent.

I'm afraid I'll have to ask you to stay at the hotel and keep your contact with people here as brief as possible for your own safety." His voice lost the smiling sound as he smiled apologetically at me. I sighed and nodded. I should have known this was going to keep haunting me.

Dean carefully parked the car in the parking lot of a small hotel outside of downtown Des Moines. The city was so tiny compared to New York that calling it a city seemed like a sad joke. It seemed grayer than I remembered—less alive. The trees reached up with grasping fingers, scratching at an unforgiving sky for warmth and light. Even though the trees were starting to sprout little buds, I couldn't see the green. The day would have been warm if the wind wasn't blowing, but dark clouds were building across the sky as the sun set. Spring snow threatened, but I didn't care.

Dean walked in front of me, his thin frame easy to follow through the empty hallways to my room. It was a nice room, nicer than anything I could have afforded, but it was still just a hotel room. I went to the closet to hang my jacket and found my things already arranged neatly. Glancing around the room, I could see small touches that could only be the work of Rachel. My mail on the table, fresh flowers in a vase by the door, my toothbrush and a red cup by the sink.

Dean handed me a card with his name and telephone number, reminding me if I needed anything to call him. "I'll bring by some pizza in an hour or so for you. What would you like?"

"Pineapple and bacon," I answered automatically.

Comfort food sounded good. He grinned and shut the heavy door softly behind him. I stood in the center of the room, suddenly lost. I didn't want to be here. I didn't want to be in New York. I wanted to be somewhere I belonged. I wanted this hole in my heart to either disappear or fill up with something that didn't hurt so much.

I slid the blonde wig off my head and onto a wig stand in the bathroom. Rachel had thought of everything. I looked at myself in the mirror. I still looked the same, brown hair, brown eyes, but I knew something must be different about me. I didn't feel like me anymore. I suddenly wanted out of my expensive clothes, out of everything that had anything to do with New York or the almost-life I had left behind.

I threw the suit on the tile floor, a sick sense of satisfaction at the expensive fabric lying in a pile. I stepped on it as I walked past. All I wanted was a pair of old sweats and a t-shirt. I dug through the drawers, but all I could find was beautiful expensive clothes from New York. I ripped them out of the drawers and off their hangers, tossing them in angry showers to the floor as I searched. I didn't want this. All I wanted was something simple, comfortable. Finally, in the bottom drawer of the last dresser, I found my ratty scrub pants and a t-shirt.

With a sob of relief I dove into the familiar fabric, feeling it rub against my skin. The hem on the pants was fraying and a hole had developed in the t-shirt, but I didn't care. Hot tears leaked down my cheeks, leaving red lines of frustration and hurt behind them.

I sat down on the bed, a raft in a sea of clothes, and cried until I passed out, exhausted.

CHAPTER TWENTY-TWO

Five days, three hours, and twenty three minutes since I left New York. I had been cooped up in the hotel room for five days, and I was ready to kill. Dean brought me whatever kind of food I wanted, and I had free reign of room service and the coffee cart in the library, provided I wore the blonde wig whenever I opened the door.

I hated it. The weather outside was slowly getting warmer, the sunshine teasing me with happiness. I went out in the hotel courtyard several times, but there was always a businessman on his phone, or a family planning their drive back through Nebraska. I wanted to be alone, not silently sharing strangers' lives, so I tended to stay in my room and pull the drapes.

I watched more TV in those few days than I had in my whole life. I suddenly understood the allure of reality TV, or at least the mind-numbing time-killing ability of it. It was at least a way to pass time while I waited for my world to settle enough that I could go back into it.

Dean kept his distance, bringing me food and movies at regular intervals. He was friendly and easy going, but he kept our relationship strictly professional. He was my bodyguard, not my friend. He had other things to do than sit in my hotel room and listen to me whine.

Rachel and I texted throughout the day, but she was busy with work. I had a feeling Jack was finding her extra tasks to keep her busy so she wouldn't remind him about me. She kept telling me that things were going to get better, but, from my lonely hotel room, the world looked desolate and gray.

I wished for the umpteenth time that I could at least tell Ashley where I was so she could come visit me, but Dean had expressly forbidden it. I couldn't tell anyone—not even my parents—that I was back in town, because anyone connected with me was probably being watched. I told him he was paranoid and crazy and he looked at me with icy blue eyes until I finally relented.

I felt lost. Without my friends or family, there was nothing in Iowa that I wanted. Without Jack and Rachel, there was nothing in New York that wanted me. I was in my home state, but I couldn't have been farther away from home if I tried.

"Celebrities Revealed! Look who is back in rehab? The troubled starlet was seen checking in-" The TV blared out, suddenly loud as a tabloid show flashed on the screen. I flopped around on the bed, trying to find the remote. "Where is Emma LaRue? Are the two lovers splitting up?"

At my name, I turned to the screen. A video of Jack carrying me out of the restaurant as the paparazzi swarmed us flashed across the screen, making my chest squeeze. Jack's eyes flashed furious as he cradled me close to him, protective and fierce. I could almost smell his cologne, the soft scent of his soap as I remembered. The void in my chest threatened to swallow me whole. I squeezed my eyes shut, blocking the tears that wanted to escape. *I'm past this*, I told myself. If I said it enough times, it would be true.

"Emma LaRue has not been seen entering the DS Oil and Gas Building for almost a week after weeks of almost nightly visits. No sightings of her, or the happy couple anywhere in New York." The screen flashed to a video of Jack in his office. Someone with a camera was in the grand entrance looking through his open office door. He looked worn and tired, dark circles under his eyes. He seemed to carry a heavy weight across his shoulders, heavier than I had ever seen. Upon seeing the camera, his eyes blazed and the door to his office slammed shut, the angry face of Jeannette filling the screen before cutting back to a picture of me smiling in Times Square. "Jack Saunders appears hard at work, so where is the lovely Emma?"

I barely recognized myself in the photograph. The hair was mine, the arms and legs were right, the clothing matched something I knew was piled on the floor in the closet, but the smile was something foreign. I had been so happy. All the joy from loving Jack radiated out of that smile, filling the picture with sunny warmth. It was only on the screen for a moment before the announcer shifted stories, and grainy pictures of a long legged blonde woman in compromising positions filled the screen.

"What are you watching?" Dean asked, stepping through the doorway. I hadn't even heard him knock, but I had given him a key. He stood with a bag of groceries, a perplexed look on his face as he watched the blurred images of a lurid sex tape flit across the screen. I finally found the remote and hit the power button.

The TV died with an electronic hiss. "Nothing worth watching," I said sitting up. He set the food down on the table and walked over to the window, pulling the drapes open. I hissed like a vampire as bright sun flooded the room.

"It is a gorgeous day outside. You haven't been out of this hotel room in over three days and—"

"I went to the courtyard on Monday!" I interjected. He gave me a look that made it very clear what he thought of that.

"The courtyard doesn't count as outside. The crab apple trees are blooming and you are within walking distance of one of the largest collections of flowering crab apple trees in the world. Arie den Boer Arboretum is just down the road. You are going to get up, get dressed, and go take a walk. Absorb nature."

"I don't wanna."

"Don't make me make you." He gave me the same

look my father used to give when I didn't want to do my chores.

I sighed and rolled off the bed. It was easier to appease him than to fight him. Besides, I hadn't been to the 'crabby-apple park' since I was a kid. I remembered that some horticulturist had collected hundreds of varieties of flowering crab apple trees and planted them in a park. My dad would take me for a picnic lunch when the trees first went into bloom until I started high school and decided it wasn't cool anymore.

Dean put the groceries in the mini fridge as I changed in the bathroom. It felt good to get out of my scrubs and into real clothes again. Just changing made the world feel a little better. I ran a brush through my hair before pulling it up into a messy bun and throwing a hat on my head. I didn't want to wear the wig. I was tired of being fake.

I stepped out and Dean did a once over, handing me a pair of sunglasses before deciding I looked nondescript enough to venture outside. I was beginning to feel excited about seeing the trees. There was a river that ran along the park, and I remembered ducklings and goslings playing in the grass under the pink and white blossoms. Dean nodded his approval as I slid on sneakers, a smile starting to form on my lips. This was the happiest I had felt since I arrived.

I got a head start out the door, knowing Dean would shadow me quietly. He was my bodyguard after all, but I was going to pretend like he wasn't there and he was going to let me. It felt a weight lift off my shoulders as I stepped out of the main lobby and into the spring sunshine.

It only took a minute to walk down to the river, following a path towards a forest of flowering trees. I could see bikes and runners working their way around the lake across the street, everyone smiling and waving in the spring sunshine.

I walked slowly, letting the sunshine warm my bones. The air was cool, but with a heat of something warmer coming, the sweet scent of apple blossoms filling my mind. The river gurgled gently as I walked, singing of the end of winter and the journey to the sea.

The path diverged from the river and headed towards the pink and white blossoming trees. I could see small flowers dancing on gentle breezes, twirling and spinning from their branches onto carpets of pink and white. Birds chirped in the trees. The world was quiet and peaceful.

I walked slowly through the trees, absorbing the sweet perfume of the flowers, and soaking in the warm sunshine. For the first time in days, I felt like things might get better. I could survive this. I didn't need Jack Saunders. In the sunshine and falling petals, I could almost believe the lie.

I wandered off the path, traipsing through the fallen petals and grass to a tree in the corner of the park. I sat down, feeling the rough bark pull at my jacket as I leaned back against it. I wished I knew how to paint, because this was something worth painting. The trees danced in swirls of pink and white, contrasting the pale blue of the sky and the dark blue of the river. Green grass peeked up through the fallen flowers and thick brown trunks rose from the ground. A gosling tottered behind its black and gray mother, trying to mimic her wobbly gait.

"You always seem to pick the spots with the best view," a deep voice said from the other side of the tree. My chest tightened and for a moment I couldn't breathe as I dared to hope. A sandy head peeked around the low gnarled branches, hazel eyes bright against the blossoms.

"I don't pick them. They pick me," I said softly. I was surprised I could speak at all. A war of emotions was waging within my head. Part of me was still angry at the hurt he had caused, part of me was afraid this was all in my mind, but most of me was lost in love. He sat down next to me, leaning against the rough tree bark.

The universe seemed to hold its breath. He was close enough to touch, our knees and shoulders barely inches from touching, yet far enough that it would require movement. I knew he was there for me, there was no other reason for him to be at Water Works Park in Iowa, but I still couldn't believe it.

"I need to apologize," he said softly, staring out at the river. A pink blossom floated down gently and landed in his hair. "My mother told me you tried to return the money when she first gave it to you. The things I said, they were cruel... and untrue."

I nodded, barely daring to blink for fear he might vanish. I couldn't speak, the words too big to even fit in my mouth. He took a deep breath.

"You've been gone less than a week and I can't get you out of my head. I can't concentrate and I don't sleep without knowing you are safe and nearby. I miss you at dinner. I can't concentrate at work because I know you won't be there." He played with a flower at his feet. "I have always been alone, but I don't want to be alone—I can't be alone without you anymore."

He turned and looked at me, his hazel eyes almost green today. They captured me, held me in their depths so that I didn't need to breathe. His hands reached for mine, and I wasn't sure which one of us was trembling more, but together we were strong.

"I love you, Emma."

I didn't think. I leaned forward and kissed him. I kissed him like it was the only thing that mattered in this world, like we were the only people in all of creation and we existed solely for this kiss. Time stood wondrously still and somehow flew by at the same time as our lips connected and my world righted itself.

"I love you too," I whispered as we broke apart. His smile rivaled the sun. I would have traded the moon and the stars for that smile. He brushed a blossom from my hair, letting his fingers then trace the line of my jaw before bringing me to him for a second kiss. If the first one was good, this one blew it out of the water. Every fiber in my being trembled with happiness.

He pulled me close to him, our bodies touching as he held me. Pink flowers floated gently to the ground, dancing around us with joy at our reunion. The sun was brighter and the sky bluer. His arms wrapped around me, filling me with warmth and joy. I leaned into him and he softly kissed my head as we looked out at the lake and the falling blossoms, the world falling back into place.

❧ ❧

EPILOGUE

The sand is warm beneath my toes, the sun shining down happily and making everything bright. A light breeze off the ocean ruffles my dress as I smile at my dad and take his arm. He looks so proud as he turns to guide me towards the water and to the man I love.

Jack stands by the ocean in white linen, apparently at ease to everyone but me. I can see the way his jaw is tightened, the slight clench in his hand and the perfect posture despite appearing at ease. He relaxes slightly as our eyes meet, the tension melting as he smiles at me like I am the most beautiful thing he has ever seen.

I'm next to Jack before I can even take a breath, my father kissing me softly on the cheek and shaking Jack's hand before leaving me. I can't stop the blush that floods my cheeks as I look at Jack, the sheer happiness radiating out of him infectious. He holds out a hand for mine, and as our hands connect, I'm not nervous anymore. My world is exactly the way it is supposed to be.

The minister begins speaking, but I'm not paying attention to him. I can hear sniffling behind me, and Mrs. Saunders keeps dotting at her eyes with a soft white handkerchief. My own mother is leaning her head to my father's shoulder, tears falling unabashedly down her face. My father's eyes are bright with tears and his feet covered in fine white sand from walking me to where I now stand.

Jack smiles and I am back to him. He is all that matters today. I can't help but smile, can't help but feel this joy flooding through me. We are two people in love, finally getting married.

Jack takes my hand and slides on a ring. It isn't big or gaudy—a simple diamond in a simple white gold setting. He promises to love me forever. I promise the same and slide a simple matching man's ring onto his left hand. I know I am shaking, but it is with love and happiness. The minister has us repeat his words, but they are just words. I am looking at Jack, our eyes telling one another more than words ever could.

I can hear cameras clicking, but I don't care. They are allowed to be here this time. I don't care how much my dress costs, what the ring looks like or what color the flowers are. Today is for me and Jack. All I care about is that those hazel eyes are holding mine. All I care about is this joy between us, this joy that is ours alone. The joy that we are choosing to share with those we love, as we are wed in truth.

SALTWATER KISSES

ABOUT THE AUTHOR

Krista Lakes is a newly turned 30 year old who recently rediscovered her passion for writing. She loves aquatic life and running marathons. She is living happily ever after with her Prince Charming and her bouncing baby boy.

Krista would love to hear from you! Please contact her at Krista.Lakes@gmail.com or like her on Facebook!

Made in the USA
Columbia, SC
20 February 2018